NICKEL
BAY NICK

NICKEL BAY NICK

DEAN PITCHFORD

G. P. PUTNAM'S SONS

AN IMPRINT OF PENGUIN GROUP (USA) INC.

G. P. PUTNAM'S SONS
An imprint of Penguin Young Readers Group
Published by The Penguin Group
Penguin Group (USA) Inc., 375 Hudson Street, New York, NY 10014, USA

USA | Canada | UK | Ireland | Australia | New Zealand | India | South Africa | China
Penguin Books Ltd, Registered Offices: 80 Strand, London WC2R 0RL, England
For more information about the Penguin Group, visit penguin.com

Library of Congress Cataloging-in-Publication Data
Pitchford, Dean.
Nickel Bay Nick / Dean Pitchford.
pages cm
Summary: When eleven-year-old Sam gets into trouble and is forced to work for
his reclusive neighbor Mr. Wells, he soon finds out that his mysterious new
acquaintance hides many secrets of his own—including one that will change Sam's life forever.
[1. Behavior—Fiction. 2. Secrets—Fiction. 3. Neighbors—Fiction. 4. Christmas—Fiction.
5. City and town life—Fiction.] I. Title.
PZ7.P644Ni 2013
[Fic]—dc23
2012048972

Published simultaneously in Canada. Printed in the United States of America.
ISBN 978-0-399-25465-9
1 3 5 7 9 10 8 6 4 2

Design by Marikka Tamura.
Text set in Century Schoolbook.
The publisher does not have any control over and does not assume any responsibility
for author or third-party websites or their content.

To Patrick Mealiffe,
whose heart beats throughout this story

CONTENTS

THE TWELVE DAYS OF CHRISTMAS

DECEMBER

SUNDAY	MONDAY	TUESDAY	WEDNESDAY	THURSDAY	FRIDAY	SATURDAY
						1
2	3	4	5	6	7	8
9	10	11	12	13	14	15
16	17	18	19	20	21	22
23	24	🎁 25 CHRISTMAS	🍬 26 1ST DAY	🍬 27 2ND DAY	🍬 28 3RD DAY	🍬 29 4TH DAY
🌲 30 5TH DAY	🌲 31 6TH DAY					

JANUARY

SUNDAY	MONDAY	TUESDAY	WEDNESDAY	THURSDAY	FRIDAY	SATURDAY
		🌲 1 7TH DAY	🌲 2 8TH DAY	☆ 3 9TH DAY	☆ 4 10TH DAY	☆ 5 11TH DAY
☆ 6 12TH DAY	7	8	9	10	11	12
13	14	15	16	17	18	19
20	21	22	23	24	25	26
27	28	29	30	31		

MISSION KEY

🍬 : RED MISSION

🌲 : GREEN MISSION

☆ : WHITE MISSION

THE STRANGER IN THE PHOTOGRAPH
December 25

Crash!

From where I'm standing in the parking lot of the condemned Nickel Bay railroad station, I hear glass from the broken window shatter as it hits the concrete floor inside. If I could get up there, close to those high windows—what is that? Twenty, thirty feet up?—I would smash them all with my fists. BAM! BAM! BAM! BAM! Glass everywhere, falling like sharp snowflakes. Instead, I do my smashing from down below, using chunks of the crumbled asphalt that's poking up through the snow at my feet.

My breath makes small, quick puffs in the night air. Despite the cold, I'm sweating. Long, wet strands of brown hair are hanging in my eyes, and I'm still panting hard from running so far so fast. I hadn't meant to head for the old depot. It's just where I happened to end up when I ran out of run.

I heft another lump of asphalt and wonder, how many

can I break in a row? Three? Four? And once I do, would I feel any better? Would I feel any less angry? Less betrayed?

You want the truth? This has got to be the Worst. Christmas. *EVER!*

And I'm including the Christmas when I was almost four, the one I spent in a hospital bed, hooked up to a hundred tubes and surrounded by racks of beeping machines. I had just had a heart transplant. Seriously. A holiday heart transplant!

And yet this Christmas is way worse. Otherwise I wouldn't be standing out here in the freezing-cold dark, shaking with fury and throwing stones.

Dad closed his shop today—the Nickel Bay Bakery and Cupcakery. He usually keeps it open on Christmas, but he's having a bad month. After Thanksgiving, he had to lay off his staff. Extend his hours. Cut his prices. But business is still lousy.

And guess who gets to help Dad out around the store.

Yup.

I've been there every day for three weeks, after school and on weekends. Sweeping floors. Washing bread pans. Folding pastry boxes. Last Saturday I folded too many, and he flipped out. "We'll never sell this many cupcakes!" he barked. "Unfold these now!" So I pushed over a stack and told him to unfold them himself, and he warned me to watch my mouth, and I shouted that he's hardly one to talk.

2

That's pretty much the way it goes these days. Slam doors, throw things, and yell, yell, yell.

Bash!

Window #2. The headlights from a lone car rake across the lot, and for a brief moment my shadow sweeps over the building's brick walls. What do I care if somebody sees me here? I've been picked up by the police enough times that I know the name of every cop in Nickel Bay. Dad reminded me of that this morning, when we were opening presents.

"I don't see anything under the tree from you to me," he said.

I snapped back, "You cut off my allowance, remember?"

"Because you stole my car, *remember?*"

Okay, wait. It's not how it sounds.

It wasn't *me* who stole the car. I'm eleven, so there's no way I'm gonna drive. I just took the keys from Dad's jacket. My friend Jaxon's the one who drove the car away from the bakery. I only went along for the ride. Me and Jaxon's girlfriend, Ivy.

And I wore my seat belt. So there.

Jaxon's fifteen. Maybe he doesn't *technically* have a driver's license, but he's already started driver's ed. He and Ivy are both older than me, but we've been a team ever since we met in the Peanut Room.

You don't know about the Peanut Room? That's where

kids at my school with medical problems have to spend lunch period. Jaxon's the only one of us who's actually allergic to peanuts. Ivy's got diabetes, so she has to take an injection at lunchtime, and with this heart thing of mine, I get stuck in there so I don't get hit in the chest out on the playground.

Ivy's fascinated by anything scientific, and she's way smarter than a lot of teachers. She gets a bad rap for being difficult, but that's only because she gets bored in class. Did I mention she's also kind of gorgeous?

Jaxon does impressions. He can mimic just about any teacher at school, but he can also make a lot of other crazy sounds. Since the first time I laughed at his impression of a spoon caught in a garbage disposal, the three of us have been hanging out.

I soon learned that even though Jaxon's dad is a rich lawyer and always buys him everything he asks for, Jaxon still loves to take things that aren't his. At first we messed around in small ways—a little shoplifting here and there. No big deal. But then we got bored. And Jaxon got inventive.

Unless you're a pale fifth-grade runt with a medical condition, you wouldn't know how awesome it feels to have a couple of eighth-graders be your friends—one who's beautiful and one who's funny. Even if the funny one sometimes suggests you do things that cross the line.

Around Thanksgiving Jaxon said he wanted to practice his driving and asked could I maybe help him borrow

4

Dad's car. How could we know that Dad had deliveries to make that afternoon? Or that he'd call the police when he saw the empty parking space in the alley behind the bakery? Even after the cops pulled us over and I explained the whole situation, they still took us down to the station.

The next day, Dad cut off my allowance. So that's why he didn't get a Christmas present.

Serves him right.

Me? I got the usual crap I get every year, the stuff Dad would have to get me anyway. But when he wraps it in holiday paper and makes me open it on Christmas morning, he calls it a "present." Socks. Underwear. A pair of jeans—*from Goodwill!* Isn't it bad enough I've got a secondhand heart?

"You have anything to say about your presents?" Dad asked.

"You call these presents?" Maybe that was mean, but he was working my last nerve.

"Watch it."

I bit out each word. "Thank. You. For. My. Presents." Then I looked over his shoulder. Twisted to peek behind the sofa. "Where is it?"

"Where's what?"

I folded my arms. "That thing I'm getting."

Dad shrugged. "I don't know what you're talking about."

"You know!" I was getting impatient. "What I asked for."

I asked for a suitcase. A small one with wheels. For my trip to see Mom. The day after Christmas, I was finally going to get away from Dad and the bakery and gray, gray Nickel Bay, and go stay with Mom until school started. It had been nine months since I last saw her.

"Your mother and I talked," Dad began carefully.

"About what?" I spit out.

"Temper," Dad warned.

"What did you say to her?" I demanded.

"We talked about"—I could tell he was choosing his words carefully—"about your behavior lately."

"What behavior?"

"*What behavior?*" Dad started to count on his fingers. "You vandalized the teachers' lounge at school."

"I accidentally broke a lamp!" I shouted. "That TV screen was already cracked."

"You spray-painted graffiti on the back wall of the Crestwood Retirement Home."

"Nobody ever goes back there!"

"You skipped seven days of school. You missed our last appointment with Mrs. Atkinson at Family Services."

"She hates me!"

"And you stole my car, which resulted in your fifth trip to police headquarters this year."

"They didn't arrest me!"

"That's because every cop in Nickel Bay has known me since high school!" Dad's voice was getting louder now. "But it's not because you didn't deserve it!"

He had run out of fingers to count on. I had run out of excuses. We stared at each other.

"So, you and Mom talked."

"We talked," he said quietly, "and we agreed that your trip was to have been a . . . reward. And we agreed that . . ."

That's where I stopped listening. Blah blah blah blah blah. Long story short? I'm not going anywhere. Two more weeks till school starts again. Two more weeks of sweeping out the bakery and fighting with my dad and hating my life.

Then he had the nerve to add, "And remember, we're going over to Lisa's for Christmas dinner."

"Forget it," I snapped.

Dad's been seeing Lisa for about a year now. She used to sell perfume at Dillard's Department Store until she got laid off.

Dad's eyes narrowed. "What did you say?"

"You heard me!" It was my turn to count on my fingers. "You ground me for two months. You stop my allowance. You make me work for no pay. You give me underwear for Christmas instead of the rolling suitcase you promised."

"I never promised you a—"

"You turn Mom against me and screw me out of my visit with her, and then what? You think I'm just gonna tag along and sit around Lisa's table with her two screaming girls and pretend we're all having a nice Christmas dinner? I'd rather drink gasoline."

Dad's never smacked me. I'm sure he's scared it would

stop my heart or something. But I can tell when he wants to, and that was one of those times.

I spent the rest of the day in my bedroom. It's hardly private, though, since Dad took the door off its hinges last month. He said I slammed it "one too many times."

Smash!

Three windows in a row. I'm on fire!

When Mom left Dad and moved away from Nickel Bay, I was three and a half, and the doctors hadn't found the hole in my heart yet.

"I've got dreams," she told Dad before she left. Mom has a really great singing voice, and over the years, she has sent me postcards saying things like, "I hope you understand, Sam, that I have to follow my star!" So far her star has taken her to Nashville and Los Angeles and tons of other places. I was always certain that, once she found success, Mom would send for me, and I'd finally get out of Nickel Bay. I'd leave Dad, with all his pathetic rules, and I'd leave the kids at school who snicker and call me Frankenstein because of the scar down my chest. I'd start a new life with Mom while she lived her dream. And maybe I'd get a dream of my own.

The last time I saw her—last spring break—I stayed with her in a dusty motel room in Memphis, where the temperature was about a billion degrees every day. To stay cool in the evenings, we sat around the half-filled swimming pool in the courtyard, and Mom sang me little pieces of songs she'd been trying to write. There was one called "I'm So Ready" that I liked a lot, so she taught me the chorus.

My heart is strong
My hands are steady
My future waits
And now I'm ready
Whoa-oh
I'm so ready

We'd sing at the top of our lungs until the motel manager poked his head out of his office and asked us to keep it down.

I haven't sung that song since I got back from Memphis.

Before Dad left for Lisa's in the late afternoon, he leaned into my bedroom. "You coming or not?"

"Not."

From across the room, I could smell that he was wearing some yucky cologne Lisa gave him. He had on his stupid Christmas sweater, the one with green holly leaves and red berries on it. Dad played football in high school before he was a fireman, which was before he worked construction and before he opened the bakery. He's still a big, muscle-y guy, and with all those leaves and berries stretched across his broad shoulders, that sweater looked extra dorky. I wasn't going to be the one to tell him.

"There's leftovers in the fridge," he said. "You know the rules: no visitors. No TV. Do not leave this house. Do I make myself clear?"

I didn't even look up. "Crystal."

He slammed the front door on the way out. See? I'm not the only one who acts like a child.

When he wants to punish me with no TV, Dad hides the remote. If he hadn't, I wouldn't have gone snooping, and if I hadn't gone snooping, I wouldn't have found the card, so what happened next is totally his fault.

The envelope was hidden in his bottom dresser drawer, behind his unmatched socks and the shoe polish rags. The postmark said Little Rock, AR.

We don't know anybody in Arkansas.

When I opened it, a picture fell out. I didn't recognize the couple in the photo—a guy with a mustache wearing a tuxedo standing next to a lady in a white dress. She was holding a bunch of flowers, with her hair piled up in curls. They both looked goofy, they were smiling so hard. Across the bottom of the photo, in gold ink, was printed OUR HAPPY DAY—DECEMBER 4.

It took a moment before it hit me that I knew the lady.

"*Mom?*" I whispered.

The note Mom had written inside the card was short. Just about how quiet and simple the wedding ceremony had been . . .

"Wedding?" I gasped.

. . . how happy she and Phil and his kids are . . .

10

Who's Phil? I wondered. *And how many kids are we talking about?*

. . . and, she wrote, how "this Christmas, as you can imagine, is hardly an ideal time for one of Sam's visits."

"Ya think?!" I blurted out in the silent bedroom. I reread the caption on the photo. OUR HAPPY DAY—DECEMBER 4.

December 4?

Mom got married, like, three weeks ago and didn't mention it? Isn't getting married the kind of thing you tell the people you love? And what about Dad? He never said a word, either!

In that moment, I hated them both. With shaking hands I crushed the wedding picture and the card, dropped them to the floor and stood up quickly.

Bad move.

Suddenly dizzy, I slumped against Dad's bedroom wall. My neck and face were burning hot, and my heart pounded in my chest, straining to pump enough blood to my head to catch up with my feelings. The few times I've passed out at school, everybody made such a big deal about it, but that's just the way my body works.

I don't remember leaving the house. I don't remember running through the snow-covered streets. I don't remember anything before that first chunk of asphalt exploded that first window.

Crash!

And now I'm up to window #4. If life were fair, I'd get

some sort of medal for hitting four targets in a row. Maybe I should be a pitcher, I think for one moment. Or maybe a quarterback. But small, scrawny kids with spare hearts don't get to be pitchers or quarterbacks. They don't get to have dreams.

My whole world is crumbling. Now with Mom married . . . and living in Little Rock . . . with that man, Phil . . . there's no chance that things will ever get better.

A sheet of newspaper blows across the empty lot and wraps around my leg. I peel off the front page of that morning's *Nickel Bay News* and read the headline:

WHERE HAVE YOU GONE, NICKEL BAY NICK???

As far back as I can remember, every year starting twelve days before Christmas, this Nickel Bay Nick character—nobody knows if it's a man or a woman, old or young, midget or monster—passes out hundred-dollar bills all over town, like a Secret Santa. At first, the newspapers and TV reporters called him—or her—Saint Nicholas . . . or Saint Nick . . . of Nickel Bay. Finally, it became simply Nickel Bay Nick.

Nick began showing up eight years ago, not long after the oldest and biggest company in the county, the Nickel Bay Furniture Works, burned down and never reopened. Without jobs to keep them here, hundreds of people moved away and tons of businesses closed. The businesses and people who stayed are still struggling to hang on.

Every year (until now), when that first hundred-dollar bill of the season shows up and everybody realizes that Nickel Bay Nick has returned, this town cheers up like you wouldn't believe. People greet each other with hugs and wave at complete strangers in the street.

But this year? No Nick. The twelve days of Christmas came and went, and with every passing day, the mood got gloomier. People walked around with slumped shoulders and scowls on their faces. Finally everybody shrugged and accepted the sad truth that even Nickel Bay Nick had deserted Nickel Bay.

I didn't think that I could feel worse than I already did. But seeing that newspaper headline reminds me that I'm not only miserable and forgotten. I'm miserable and forgotten in the most miserable and forgotten place on earth.

Then I hear the police siren. Somebody . . . maybe the headlights that drove by five minutes ago? . . . somebody must've ratted me out. I take my last shot, but my heart's not in it anymore. My chunk of asphalt flies too high, thumps against the eaves and drops with a thud into the snow.

I flip up the hood of my sweatshirt and start running.

THE MONSTER IN THE WINDOW

Cutting across the abandoned train tracks, I pass the charred remains of the Nickel Bay Furniture Works. On the night the fire tore through the main factory and leapt to the warehouses, I was home asleep, but Dad—who was still a fireman then—got the alarm. He raced down to join the rest of the Nickel Bay Fire Department in trying to stop the blaze, but with high winds spreading the flames, there wasn't anything they could do to save the Furniture Works.

What a waste! I think as I race past the skeletons of the snow-covered buildings. All this time gone by and the town still hasn't cleared the lot. Or tried to start again.

But there's decay everywhere in Nickel Bay. The WALK/ DON'T WALK signs are burned out at almost every corner. Playgrounds are chained up and there are vacant storefronts on every block. Even in what used to be the fancy part of town, over where a lot of the big, modern houses with their swimming pools sit empty, the potholes in the streets keep getting wider and deeper.

When I zig onto Sherwood Avenue, I'm only a block away from our dead-end street, Pegasus Lane. *If I can just get that far,* I'm thinking, *if I can just disappear around that corner, I'll be okay.* But when that wailing squad car squeals onto Sherwood, flashing its red and blues behind me, I panic and take a detour I've never taken before.

I jump the fence at Mr. Wells's house.

Mr. Wells lives alone on the corner of Sherwood Avenue and Pegasus Lane. Some folks think he's a snob because he doesn't wave to his neighbors, but every Christmas he strings lights all over his big old house and the two fifty-foot evergreens in his front yard. Under the trees he stacks giant, brightly wrapped boxes. The *Nickel Bay News* actually put a picture of Mr. Wells's yard on its front page once.

Using a garbage can as a springboard, I vault over Mr. Wells's wrought-iron fence and land in a crouch on his front lawn. Careful not to make footprints, I slink to the edge of the front porch and climb up on the railing, from which I'm able to reach a low-hanging branch of one of the evergreens. Christmas lights twinkle all around me as I climb until I'm level with the third floor of the house. Then I tuck my body into a tight ball and hang on for dear life.

The police turn down Pegasus Lane, but I know they'll be back. After all, it *is* a dead end. A minute passes. Another minute. Sure enough, here they come.

Screech! In front of Mr. Wells's house, a cop jumps from the squad car and switches on his flashlight. Even from up where I am, I can tell it's Officer Evan. He's slapped me in handcuffs a few times. His flashlight beam rakes across the lawn and begins climbing the front of the house. When the ray of light cuts through the branches and brushes across my left shoe, I hold my breath and squeeze closer to the tree trunk.

Just then, a switch gets flipped and the front yard lights up like a ballpark. Luckily, the floodlights are shining down from the second floor, so I'm up in the shadows.

From my position, I can't see Mr. Wells below me on his front porch, but I can hear him asking something like, ". . . problem, Officer?" Talking through the fence, Officer Evan gestures in the direction of the train station and toward the dead end of Pegasus Lane. Scattered words like "broken windows" and "act of vandalism" drift up to me. As they talk, Officer Evan continues to run his flashlight over the yard and the house, never coming close to my hiding place. Finally he tips his hat to Mr. Wells and drives off.

The front door shuts. Porch lights and floodlights snap off. Up where I am, the world is weirdly quiet. It's only then that I realize my legs, wrapped around the tree trunk, are shaking with cold, and my fingers are frozen in the shape of a claw. To restore blood circulation, I move slowly, twisting, unfolding. Over one shoulder I notice the string of Christmas lights nailed along the third-floor eaves. You'd never be able to tell from down on the ground, but up this close I can see that each light is an angel with a halo and wings.

Leaning away from the trunk, I stretch out a hand to take hold of one and get a better look at it. This little guy's wearing a choir robe, and his mouth is a perfect circle, like he's singing the "O" in "O Little Town of Bethlehem." I know it sounds lame, but holding that glowing angel in my hand is the first thing that makes me smile all day. Then I look up.

What happens next is like something out of a nightmare.

One moment I am seeing my reflection in a darkened third-story window, and in the next moment . . .

RARARARARARRR! RAAR! RAAR! RAAR! RAAR!

A huge, furry monster slams up against the glass, snarling just inches from my face, his jaws dripping with saliva, his black tongue lashing out! I scream and recoil. As I lose my grip on the tree trunk I'm straddling, my hand clamps tightly around the angel light, and I start to fall.

Down, down, down, I bounce from one snow-covered limb to another, dragging the string of Christmas lights with me. From above, I hear the ri-i-i-ipping noise of metal scraping against wood, and somewhere along the way, I let go of the angel. Every branch I drop onto breaks my fall a little, and then what really saves me from a crash landing on the cold, hard ground is that stack of fake Christmas presents.

Fortunately, the boxes are all empty, so they just collapse under my body with a big *ooof!* I roll off the pile of crushed cardboard and out from under the tree. For a moment I lie there under the starry sky, covered in snow and pine needles. I'm stunned that I've fallen so far but don't seem to be dead. The silence that follows my landing is abruptly broken by a rattling, clanking, smashing noise. I look up, and my heart leaps to my throat.

The glowing choirboy I hung on to was attached to a long string of his angel buddies. And that cord, until just seconds before, had been hammered into a wood beam supporting the steel rain gutter along the roof's edge. Now all of that—the holiday lights, the broken tree branches, the wood beam and a ten-foot section of gutter—are falling.

And the only thing between them and the frozen ground is my head.

I don't even have time to scream before I roll aside. A split second later, the beam harpoons the exact place my head had been. A few more crashes and bashes follow as more branches fall, and clumps of snow shower down over the wreckage. I lie panting on the front lawn, disoriented and terrified. I slip a hand into my jacket and am relieved to find that my heart is still beating. Suddenly, the porch light flares. Locks unlatch—one! two! three!—and the heavy front door swings open again.

Flipping over onto my stomach, I try to stand, but my sneakers slip all over the snow-dusted earth. Suddenly, two powerful hands clamp on my shoulders and squeeze. Like a rag doll, I'm spun around to face Mr. Wells's front porch.

Where Mr. Wells sits. In a wheelchair.

His right leg is covered—hip to ankle—by a white plaster cast that's supported by a metal brace extending from the chair. His square jaw clenches as he whips off a pair of black-rimmed glasses to glare at me with piercing gray eyes. In his left hand he holds the collar of a large, bushy dog—the same monster that lunged at me in the upstairs window. The dog is black and gray, with a massive head and an army of really white, really sharp teeth, which he's snapping in my direction.

RAAR! RAAR! RAAR! RAAR!

The sight of them both is so startling that it takes me a few moments to wonder, *Hey! If Mr. Wells is sitting in front of me in a wheelchair, who's holding me from behind?* I swivel my head to see a hulking stranger pinning my arms back. Six feet, maybe six and a half feet, tall. Jet-black hair. Almond-shaped eyes. Shoulders the size of a refrigerator.

"Lemme go!" I demand, but he only squeezes harder. So I yell louder, "LET ME GO!" My words die in the night air. I stop struggling and turn back to Mr. Wells, thrusting my chin out defiantly.

Slowly, Mr. Wells leans forward. "It seems," he says quietly, "that you've broken my house."

THE WEIRDO ON THE CORNER

I stand panting in the cold, waiting for Mr. Wells to say something else. That's when I realize that the hulk behind me is running his hands down my back, squeezing my arms, inspecting my fingers.

"Hey!" I snap, pulling back. "Cut it out!"

"Sakata-san," Mr. Wells says. He nods, and the goon drops my hand.

"You will refer to this gentleman as *Doctor* Sakata," Mr. Wells says. "He is trained in many healing arts and deserves your total respect."

"I don't like people touching me," I say. "*Especially* doctors."

"Dr. Sakata is merely checking you for broken bones or any other injuries." He rolls his wheelchair to the edge of the porch and glances up the side of his house. "After all, you fell from a great height."

"Okay, lookit!" I flap my arms and legs like a spastic scarecrow. "See? Nothing broken. Can I go?"

"*Go?*" The word explodes from Mr. Wells's mouth. He waves a hand at the pile of mangled tree branches, crushed boxes, Christmas lights, rain gutter and roof shingles scattered across his front lawn. "You're not going anywhere until we discuss this."

He says something in a foreign language to Dr. Sakata, who steps around me, climbs the porch steps and enters the house. With him gone, I realize I could make a break for it. Glancing back, I try to calculate the distance between me and the fence.

"Don't even think about it, Sam."

I whip around. "How do you know my name?"

Mr. Wells snorts. "I've lived here, what? Seven or eight years? Don't you think that in all that time I would learn the names of my neighbors? Especially the neighbor who bashed in my mailbox with a baseball bat, not once but twice?"

I blink in surprise. How did he know that was me? Both times?

"Wouldn't I know the identity of the neighbor who shot out my porch lights with a BB gun? Or threw the carcass of a skunk into my yard on Halloween?" Mr. Wells shakes his head and surveys the mess I've made. "Sam, let me ask you something: Do you really enjoy being such a screwup?"

Before I let loose and tell Mr. Wells where he can shove his question, my cell phone rings.

"Hold on," I order Mr. Wells, and I flip open my cell. I already know who's calling. "What?" I bark.

Dad only has me carry a cell phone for one reason. Twice a day—at seven thirty in the morning and seven thirty at night—I have to take my pill. The pill I've been taking ever since I got my new heart. The same pill I'll keep taking for the rest of my life.

Dad asks a single question, and I totally lose it. "*Where am I?* I'm right where you told me to stay!" And before he can respond, I announce, "I know. Seven thirty. Gotta swallow," and I snap the phone shut.

As I'm talking, Dr. Sakata comes out of the house carrying a steaming mug. Now he stands beside me in silence. I look to Mr. Wells and point to the cell phone. "My dad."

"Mm." Mr. Wells nods. "You always speak to your father like that?"

"Like what?"

"Lying about where you are? And so rudely?"

"That's how we talk." I shove my hand into my jeans and dig out the tiny plastic baggie holding the pill. "I gotta take this."

"Right now?"

"Twice a day."

Mr. Wells nods.

"You got any water?" I ask.

"Dr. Sakata has prepared a special tea for you."

"I don't drink tea."

"I'm not being sociable," Mr. Wells says. "It's an herbal mixture, specially blended to work on muscles and joints. You may not feel like anything's wrong right now, but unless you drink the tea, you will wake up tomorrow morning and be shocked to discover what you've just put your body through."

"I really only need water."

Mr. Wells's eyebrows shoot up. "Do you realize who you're talking to? You're speaking to the neighbor whose property you have just vandalized. The neighbor who has the Nickel Bay Police Department on speed dial," he says, picking up a phone from his lap. "And I am telling you to *drink the tea!*"

"Okay, okay, okay. Jeez." I hold up both hands. "Don't have a coronary." Taking the mug from Dr. Sakata, I blow on the hot liquid. It smells like dishwater.

I want to gag.

Mr. Wells and Dr. Sakata watch me intently. Even the big bad dog has stopped snarling and is staring at me with beady black eyes.

"We can wait all night," Mr. Wells says smoothly.

With a groan of disgust I toss the pill to the back of my throat and take a quick sip of the stinky tea. It may smell bad, but guess what?

It tastes even worse.

"BLECCCCH!" I choke, twisting my face into about a thousand wrinkles. "Are you trying to poison me?"

"Poison you?" Mr. Wells seems amused by my question. He turns to Dr. Sakata, says something in that foreign language, and they both laugh. I don't like the sound of their laughter.

"If I wanted to poison you, Sam Brattle, I wouldn't do it on the front lawn of my home, in full view of my neighbors. If I wanted to poison you and be absolutely certain you'd keel over far away from my property, I would do it correctly. Cleanly." He folds his hands and speaks in low tones. "There's a flowering vine found only in one rain forest on the Indonesian island of Sumatra. From the root of that vine, the natives extract a deadly syrup they call 'dragon's kiss.' It's a slow-acting poison, so it's very hard to trace." He pats his hands together happily. "Yes! I could feed you some dragon's kiss tea and send you home, where, after an hour or so, you'd start to experience excruciating stomach cramps. Blinding pain would pierce the base of your skull like a serrated knife. You'd be dead within seconds. That is *if* I wanted to poison you. But, no, that's not my intention tonight." He sits back in his chair and smiles. "And, Sam, for goodness' sake, close your mouth."

I realize I'm standing there with my jaw flapping down like a busted mailbox door.

"Wait here," Mr. Wells orders. He turns to his dog and says something like, "Hoko! KO-ra!" and immediately the mutt sits. With that, Mr. Wells spins around and wheels into the house.

Dr. Sakata's big mitt closes around the cup in my hand. He climbs the front steps and stands at attention next to the dog. We stay like that—them glaring at me, me glaring back—for what seems like ten minutes. Finally Mr. Wells rolls out the front door and up to the edge of the porch. He looks down at me and says, "Be here tomorrow morning at eight o'clock."

"For what?"

"This yard isn't going to clean itself." Mr. Wells waves a hand in every direction. "You don't walk away from this kind of destruction. Or do you? Because if you try, I can make a call." He wags his phone.

"I'll be here," I mumble.

"And bring your father."

"Why?" I cry out. "He doesn't have to know."

"Oh, Sam." Mr. Wells shakes his head. "Did you think that you could pull something like this and not tell your father?" From his lap he lifts a large brown envelope. "And when your father wonders who this neighbor is who wants to meet him, have him open this."

I reach for the envelope, but he pulls it back. "Only your father is to open this envelope. Do I make myself clear?"

"Crystal," I snap.

He lowers the envelope within my reach and I grab it.

"Now go home. Only this time, please use the proper exit." He points a remote control across the yard at the iron gate on Pegasus Lane. I hear a *click!* and the gate swings open. "And please have your father bring that envelope back with everything in it," Mr. Wells adds. "The contents have enormous sentimental value."

"Whatever," I grunt before I turn and walk off. Once I'm through the gate, I look back at the porch where Mr. Wells, Dr. Sakata and that humongous dog stare after me.

Didn't I tell you? Worst. Christmas. Ever.

THE SECRET IN THE ENVELOPE

When Dad finally gets back from Lisa's Christmas dinner, I'm sitting at the kitchen table, smoothing out Mom's wedding announcement and the photo. I figure they'll be good conversation starters.

As Dad walks through the front door and stomps the snow off his boots, he calls out, "You gotta see what happened to Mr. Wells's place down at the corner. Looks like that Christmas tree display of his got hit by a hurricane."

When he enters the kitchen and sees me with Mom's stuff, he freezes. It's so quiet we can hear the ticking of the kitchen clock. Finally Dad pulls out a chair and sits opposite me.

"I didn't know when to tell you," he says.

"Obviously."

"Sam, look—your mom and me, we have a complicated relationship. Since the divorce, I don't always tell you everything that's going on with us. Or with her." He picks up the wedding photo. "I wanted to tell you about this the day it came, I really did. But that was a few weeks back, the same day you were running that fever, remember?"

Because of the business with my heart and my pills, Dad's always worrying about me getting infections. And he gets everybody else worried, too. Like during flu season, if a teacher sees my cheeks are even a little pink, I get sent to the school nurse, who doesn't even bother with a thermometer before she's dialing Dad to come pick me up.

"And the day after that was our monthly meeting with Family Services," Dad says. "I know how Mrs. Atkinson always stresses you out."

After my fourth or fifth arrest, the judge made us go for counseling down at Family Services in Town Hall. Mrs. Atkinson—who's always got dandruff on her shoulders and a pencil stuck in her hair bun—tries to get me and Dad to "open up" and "share." What a joke! We always wind up yelling at each other for fifty minutes while Mrs. Atkinson scribbles like mad on her notepad.

"Even after I reminded you about the appointment," Dad continues, "you *still* forgot about it. I got so upset and angry that I was tempted to tell you about your mom right then, but I didn't want to use the news about her wedding to hurt you, so . . ." He shrugs. "I was hoping to find the right time. Sometime when you and I weren't at each other's throats, when we could discuss this calmly. But lately it seems like all we do is fight."

I don't disagree.

He points to the wedding picture. "You want to talk about this? Mom's new family?"

I shake my head and look away. The pain of the Mom situation is alternating with the terror I'm feeling about discussing Mr. Wells. Just then, my cell phone blasts Jaxon's ring tone. I pull it out and move to push the connect button.

"Don't you dare," Dad says, raising a warning finger. "Jaxon can call back."

Dad doesn't like me hanging out with Jaxon. Ivy, he's okay with, ever since she won the eighth-grade science fair with a project about yeast and solar energy that I never did understand. But he calls Jaxon "a bad influence."

Normally I'd ignore Dad and take Jaxon's call anyway, but with Mr. Wells's brown envelope waiting in my lap, I realize that I'd better not risk it. I make a big deal of snapping my phone shut.

"Thank you," Dad says.

I lay the big envelope down and slide it across the table.

"What's this?" Dad leans forward and reads the return address. "*Mister Herbert Wells.*" He looks up and jerks a thumb over his shoulder. "That Mr. Wells? Down on Sherwood? Did he come by?" When he reaches for the envelope, I put a hand on top of his.

"Before you open that, you should know," I say carefully, "Mr. Wells wants me to come work for him tomorrow morning."

"He what? Why?" Dad's face goes slack. "Oh, don't tell me." He sits back and moans. "Sam. Did you have something to do with that . . . that disaster in his yard?"

I stare back, unblinking. Dad puts two and two together and comes up with four. "I thought I told you to stay in the house!" he wails.

"I did! But then I saw these"—I point to Mom's stuff—"and I felt like I needed a little air."

That takes the wind out of his sails. We've both got reasons to be upset.

"How exactly did you destroy Mr. Wells's front yard?" Dad asks.

"I climbed one of his Christmas trees," I say with a shrug, "and I may have accidentally broken off a few branches."

"*May have?*"

"It's possible. When I fell."

Dad sits up. "You fell out of a tree?"

"Only a little ways," I lie.

"Are you hurt?"

"Do I look hurt?"

After a few more seconds, Dad sighs, and I know the worst is past. This is not the right moment, I decide, to mention the train station windows or the police chase or the gutter I tore off Mr. Wells's house.

Dad pulls his chair up to the table. "Who is this guy, Herbert Wells?" he wonders, picking up the envelope. "And what is he sending me?"

"He told me to give that to you so you can see who I'm going to be working for." Before he rips the envelope flap, I stop him with, "Oh, you better not tear it." I slide a butter knife across the table. "Mr. Wells wants you to return that envelope. When you meet him tomorrow."

"He wants to meet me tomorrow?"

I nod. "At eight."

"*Eight?* Oh, Sam." Dad groans, rubbing his forehead. "That's right when I've got to mix the breads and start the ovens."

"I know," I mutter as he continues.

"And remember, we didn't have Nickel Bay Nick to sprinkle holiday cheer all over town this year! So business is hurting. Everybody's hurting."

I bite my lip and shrug. "Mr. Wells said eight o'clock."

With a sigh, Dad takes the knife, carefully slices open the envelope and draws out a stack of photographs. The large size. When he sees the first picture, Dad's eyebrows tilt in a kind of "*Huh?*" direction.

"What is it?" I ask, but Dad doesn't answer. Instead, he slides that photo to the bottom of the pile, and when he sees the second one, his eyes get bigger. That continues for the third and fourth and by the time he hits the fifth photo, his eyes are the size of hubcaps.

"What? Is something wrong?"

"No . . . no . . . ," Dad mumbles as if he's been hypnotized.

"What are they, then?"

Dad deals the photos out in front of me like we're playing

cards. In all of them, Mr. Wells is shaking hands with a different man, and in each one, they're standing in front of an American flag. I squint at the faces. A couple of the hand-shakers look familiar, but I'm not exactly sure what I'm looking at.

"Who are these guys?"

"These . . . ," Dad says slowly, "are the last five presidents of the United States."

I look again. Dad's right.

"Whoa." I exhale. "I wonder why Mr. Wells wanted you to see these."

"I think he's sending us a message."

"What kind of message?"

"Our neighbor is gently but firmly telling us that he's not somebody we want to mess with."

I don't get much sleep that night. Every time I start to nod off, I see that monster dog yapping at the windowpane, and I jolt awake. And when I'm not remembering that, I'm seeing the photo of Mom, smiling from under her wedding hair. Standing next to Phil.

Dad tells me that when I was little, Mom and I used to play hide-and-seek at our old house, the one where we lived when we were a family. Sometimes if she'd hide and I couldn't find her, I would panic and start crying. And then Mom would come racing out of her hiding place and scoop me up in her arms.

"What's the matter?" she used to ask with a laugh.

"I . . . thought . . . I . . . lost . . . you," I would gasp between sobs.

"Never!" she always assured me as she danced us
around the room. "You will never, ever lose me."

But I have. I've pretty much lost Mom, I realize, to her
new family. Maybe there will be visits, but she's somebody else's wife now. Somebody else's mom. Not really
mine. Not anymore.

THE HIGH COST OF FALLING

December 26

The next morning, Dad's banging around in the kitchen. Crawling out of bed, I'm surprised I don't hurt more than I do. Sure, there're bruises and scratches and some stiffness here and there, but after running from the cops, after all the climbing and falling and crash-landing of the night before, I was expecting to feel like hammered dog meat. It's not until I'm pulling on my jeans and sweatshirt that I remember drinking Dr. Sakata's stinky tea. *Did it work?* I wonder. *Does the big guy actually know what he's doing?*

Dad and I eat breakfast in silence, and I take my pill without him having to remind me. "Got your gloves?" he asks before we leave, and I remind him, "Why? We're only going to the corner."

It's cold and clear outside. As we walk up to Mr. Wells's house, a truck that says REGAL ROOFING on its side pulls out, and an iron gate slides back across the driveway.

Dad rings the intercom at the front yard entrance, and Mr. Wells's voice crackles. "Meet me at the porch." The buzzer buzzes, and as the gate swings open, Dad looks to me. Together we take a deep breath and enter.

In the light of day, my "accident" looks worse than it did the night before. Strands of Christmas lights, lengths of twisted gutter and roof shingles are flung all over the lawn. Tree branches are snapped, and all the oversize Christmas presents that broke my fall are crushed. Dad whispers out of the corner of his mouth, "That's quite a mess . . . even for you." Before I can respond, the big oak front door creaks open, and Dr. Sakata pushes Mr. Wells's wheelchair to the edge of the porch. The demon dog isn't with them.

"Herbert Wells," Mr. Wells says, extending a hand. Dad reaches up, and they shake.

"Dwight Brattle," Dad says before returning to my side.

"And this"—Mr. Wells nods behind his chair—"is my physician, Dr. Sakata." Dad starts to step forward again, but when Dr. Sakata bows, Dad glances at me, confused. Finally, awkwardly, he bows back.

"Ordinarily I would say 'Good to meet you,'" Mr. Wells begins, "but under the circumstances . . ." He stops and nods toward his front lawn.

"Yeah, yeah, of course," Dad says. "I'm sorry about this. We"—he quickly points a finger back and forth between him and me—"we are *very* sorry about this. Sam is . . . devastated!"

Devastated? I never said that.

"He's ready to do whatever's necessary to make things right," Dad offers.

"Well, Sam can start with the cleanup out here," Mr. Wells says, "but that will hardly begin to compensate me for the damages."

"No . . . no, I wouldn't think so," says Dad.

I look around, and realizing how much work I'm facing, my stomach does a backflip.

"I've already had the roofers here this morning," Mr. Wells says, slipping on his glasses and studying a piece of paper in his hand. "Just to give me an estimate, you understand?"

"Totally," Dad agrees.

"The roof repairs alone are . . . my, my . . ." Mr. Wells wags his head, like he can't believe what he's reading. "And that's not including the gutter work. Plus, the evergreen will have to be trimmed and reshaped. My decorations will have to be replaced. So much to do." He removes his glasses and looks down at us. "In other words, this was no cheap prank."

"No, sir, I understand," Dad mutters.

"Call me Herbert, please," Mr. Wells says. "After all, we *are* neighbors."

Dad runs a hand through his hair. "Look . . . uh . . .

Herbert . . . ," he stammers, "financially speaking, right now, things are kinda bad. I can't afford everything immediately, but maybe we could work out some sort of repayment schedule?"

In Dad's voice I hear a combination of worry . . . and pleading. It's something I've never heard from him before, and for the first time since last night's fiasco, I feel pretty awful about what I've done.

Mr. Wells purses his lips and studies us from his perch up there on his porch. "I have a proposition to make."

Dad tilts his head. "A proposition?"

Mr. Wells thumps the plaster cast on his leg. "I broke my leg at Thanksgiving."

"Sorry to hear that," Dad says quickly.

Mr. Wells waves a hand. "Ice on the back stairs. It was my own fault. Anyway, I called my old friend Dr. Sakata"—hearing his name, the big guy nods—"and asked him to come to Nickel Bay and lend a hand. In a house this size, with all these stairs, the simplest task becomes a nightmare."

Dad grunts in understanding.

"Then I figured that if I'm going to be stuck in this wheelchair, I might as well spend my time profitably. So I've begun organizing. Boxes in the attic. Papers in the basement. A lifetime of clutter, you know what I'm saying?"

"Do I ever." Dad nods.

"Sam?" Mr. Wells turns to me. "You *do* know your alphabet, don't you?"

"My what?" I can't figure out what Mr. Wells is getting at.

"Your alphabet."

"You know the alphabet," Dad prompts me. "A, B, C, D . . ."

"Yeah, yeah, yeah. L, M, N, O, Z," I snap. "Why?"

"Well, if you can carry boxes up and down stairs and arrange files alphabetically," Mr. Wells explains, "I will pay you the minimum hourly wage and apply your earnings to my repair bills as they come in. And at the end of your Christmas break, we will consider our accounts settled. Are we agreed?"

I panic. "But, my dad . . . ," I say, "he needs me at his store!"

"I'll manage!" Dad says louder.

"Wonderful!" Mr. Wells announces. "Sam can start immediately."

Mr. Wells closes the discussion with a nod and indicates to Dr. Sakata to wheel him back inside.

"Wait a second," Dad calls out, and offers up the brown envelope of photographs. "You wanted these back?"

"Ah. Thank you," Mr. Wells says. Dr. Sakata reaches down to take the package from Dad.

"Herbert, I have to ask . . . ," Dad blurts out.

"Yes?" Mr. Wells replies.

I can see Dad trying to figure out how to phrase his

question. "Those photographs . . . I mean . . . you seem to know some important men. And they seem to know you."

"You want to know about my career," Mr. Wells says. "What I did before retirement?"

Dad snaps his fingers. "Exactly!"

"Let's just say that I worked in Foreign Services. For our country."

"Sounds . . . interesting," Dad says.

"It was never dull." Mr. Wells smiles mysteriously.

Dad's not a nosy person, but I could tell that he was itching to know more. And to tell the truth, so was I. Dad starts to ask, "Where did you . . . ?"

"Work?" Mr. Wells finishes the question. "Asia, mostly. Cambodia, Vietnam, China, Indonesia. And a half dozen other countries."

A sudden thought hits me. "So *that's* how you know about that poison!"

Dad looks to me. "What poison?"

"Sam and I," Mr. Wells interrupts, "we were discussing exotic botanicals of Southeast Asia last evening. My wife, Bernice, used to say . . ."

"Oh, you were married?" Dad asks.

"Thirty-seven years. That's a long time to be happy." For the first time since I met him, I see Mr. Wells's jaw unclench. His eyes unfocus, like he's watching a video playing inside his brain. "Bernice was fearless. Certainly more fearless than I. Orders would come down from the State Department that we'd been reassigned, and she'd

40

have the house packed within the hour. From the biggest modern cities in Asia to the most remote jungles of Thailand or India, she embraced every challenge."

"Sounds like quite a woman," Dad says. "Did you have any kids?"

Mr. Wells takes a deep breath and draws himself up in his chair. "A boy and a girl, yes. My daughter married an Australian and lives there now. And my son . . ." Mr. Wells hesitates, then smiles at Dad. "Well, I don't have to tell you." He nods in my direction. "Sons can be a handful."

"No argument there." Dad laughs, and I can tell that he likes this guy. He raises a hand like he's in a classroom. "Oh, one more thing?"

"Yes, Dwight."

Dad drops his hand and wipes it on his pant leg. "Sam has . . . uh . . . a medical issue."

"Oh?"

I can see Dad struggling to find the right words, so I save him the trouble.

"I got a heart transplant when I was nearly four. Got a big scar from here"—I place one finger at my navel—"to here." I point another finger at my upper rib cage. "That's why I'm small for my age. And as white as rice."

"And the medicine," Dad prompts me.

But Mr. Wells interjects, "Oh, I know about the pills, Dwight. Twice a day, right?"

That catches Dad by surprise. That his neighbor knows about my medication schedule.

"Right," Dad mutters. "Seven thirty a.m. and seven thirty p.m."

"And don't worry about meals," Mr. Wells says. "Dr. Sakata is an exceptional chef."

My stomach seizes, remembering the pukey tea he'd made for me the night before. Am I supposed to eat garbage like that every day until school starts again?

"Well, good, he's all yours, Herbert," Dad says, checking his watch. "Now, if you'll excuse me, I have to go start my ovens."

And just like that, he turns and heads down the walkway. I can't believe it! Without a second thought, he delivers me into slavery! Behind me, I hear the gate buzz open and then snap shut. When I raise my chin, I find Mr. Wells and Dr. Sakata staring down.

For a second, I consider running, but I've run everywhere there is to run in Nickel Bay, and all I get is short of breath.

And a pain in my chest.

THE BIG THREAT OF BLACKMAIL

For the next few hours I hack up mangled branches and cut the giant, flattened cardboard gift boxes into pieces small enough to stomp into the garbage bins that Dr. Sakata keeps rolling out. Every few minutes I have to stop to blow on my freezing fingers. Now I wish I hadn't scoffed at Dad when he asked, "Got your gloves?" this morning.

I can be so dumb sometimes.

As I work, I look around and notice for the first time just how big Mr. Wells's place actually is. All these years of peering in through his wrought-iron fence, I'd never noticed that there's a lot more to the house than you can see from the street. A three-story tower at one corner has an upside-down ice-cream-cone-shaped roof, and the rooms in that tower are hidden by trees. The wide front porch wraps around and runs down the side of the house toward a backyard.

A hundred years ago, when people in Nickel Bay had money and dreams, a lot of these big houses got built along Sherwood Avenue. Now Mr. Wells's place is the only one left, although I don't know why one person would want to live here alone. Even if he does have a humongous dog.

After a few hours, Dr. Sakata backs out of the driveway in Mr. Wells's SUV. Twenty minutes later he returns and crosses the lawn to where I'm raking up tree branches. He pulls a pair of black leather gloves from a small shopping bag, and without saying a word, he grabs my right hand off the rake and holds it up against a glove for comparison.

I start to complain, "Hey, what're you . . . ?" but then I see that my hand and the glove are the same size. Dr. Sakata breaks the plastic tab that joins the gloves together and holds them out.

"For me?" I ask. "Seriously?"

I glance toward the house. In a window on the first floor, the corner of a curtain quickly drops, and I know I've caught Mr. Wells watching us. As I take the gloves from Dr. Sakata, I feel I should say something, maybe thank him, but I doubt he'll understand a word out of my mouth. So I just bow, and he bows back.

More hours go by. My stomach's starting to grumble when Dr. Sakata appears and leads me around the side of the house. Inside the service porch, Dr. Sakata takes off his shoes and indicates that I should do the same. That's when I realize how muddy and messy I've gotten doing my work. Once I peel off my jacket and new gloves and hang them on a wall hook, I follow Dr. Sakata into the kitchen.

Did I say "kitchen"? It's more like an airplane hangar! Old wood cabinets line the room. There's a massive stove and a refrigerator as big as a garage. A football team could run sprints in here and never bump into one another. Behind me, I hear a low growl. I turn and almost scream like a girl.

From a large crate in the corner of the room, the demon dog stares out, his head hanging low and his eyes glowing with hatred and hunger. I'm horrified to notice that the door is open, but before he can leap up and tear my throat out, Dr. Sakata snaps, "Hoko!" and the growling stops.

Hoko! I get it now. The monster's name is Hoko.

"KO-ra!" barks Dr. Sakata.

The beast sits and yawns.

KO-ra? Maybe that means "stop growling!" or "don't eat the pale little boy." Whatever it is, I gotta remember that. *KO-ra!* could come in handy.

Dr. Sakata has set a single place at the kitchen table with a bowl of tomato soup, a grilled cheese sandwich and a cup of tea. He sure has a thing for tea. The doctor gestures for me to sit and eat, and once I pull my chair up to the table, he starts to leave.

"Hey!" I jerk my head toward Hoko, who's watching me like I'm his lunch. Dr. Sakata seems to understand my concern. He tears a small corner from my sandwich, holds it toward Hoko and then quickly snatches it back, wagging a "no! no! no!" finger at me.

"Oh, don't worry," I assure him. "I'm not gonna feed the dog."

Dr. Sakata pops the sandwich bit in his mouth and walks out. Left alone under the watchful gaze of Hoko, I start to eat. I gotta admit my soup and sandwich are pretty good. I even sip the tea. Next thing you know, I've finished the whole cup. My stomach makes gurgling noises, and Hoko licks his lips.

Out of boredom, I begin to study my surroundings. Behind me on a countertop a rubber-banded stack of mail sits unopened. I'm suddenly seized with curiosity about the interests and activities of my odd neighbor, so I tilt my chair back and extend an arm.

But a threatening snarl from Hoko puts an end to that plan.

A half hour goes by. Then forty-five minutes. I know this because there's a big clock hanging over the sink, tick, tick, ticking. An hour passes before Dr. Sakata returns, clears my dishes and indicates, *Come.* With Hoko trotting behind me, we exit the kitchen and enter a long hallway.

Then it happens. "Uh, excuse me?" I call out. When Dr. Sakata turns, I wince and squeeze my knees together, the universal sign for "gotta go!" Halfway down the corridor, Dr. Sakata opens a door. I peek into a little bathroom and exhale with relief.

Once I'm done there, we continue down the hall, passing through a big, fancy dining room and into a massive entry with the front door on one side and, on the other, a whopping staircase that spirals up to the second and third floors. We come to a stop in front of a pair of giant sliding oak doors. Dr. Sakata rolls one open and steps aside to allow me to enter.

Once I do, I feel like I'm not in Nickel Bay anymore.

Mr. Wells's living room looks as if it's been taken from some faraway palace and reassembled here. Dozens of large rugs, woven with thousands of colors, overlap, covering the entire floor. Hanging on one wall are old, faded fabrics embroidered with scenes of stampeding horses, clashing armies and ships tossing at sea. On the wall to my right, all sorts of old weapons are mounted. Daggers. Pistols. Swords. And the wall behind me is covered with dozens of masks, all painted and twisted into freaky expressions.

Heavy curtains frame the windows, and even though they're tied back, they still block out a lot of the afternoon sunlight. Around the room, candles flicker from lanterns shaped like owls and warriors and turtles. In opposite corners stand two tall fountains in which water is splashing down into dark pools. Everywhere I look there are statues of ladies in veils and men in robes carved out of polished

47

black rock or dark green jade, some of them almost as tall as me. Across the room, behind a massive desk flanked by two wooden elephants, Mr. Wells sits. The glow from a computer screen casts a blue tint on his face.

I can't help myself. "Wow," I gasp.

Mr. Wells looks over the rim of his glasses.

"Ah, yes. Sam." He stabs with a ballpoint pen at a chair in front of his desk. "Sit."

But I'm still freaking out. "Where'd you get all this stuff?"

"I'll be asking the questions here," Mr. Wells says, real snippy-like.

Fine. Be like that. I don't want to be your friend anyway. I don't really say that. I just think it.

And I sit.

Mr. Wells stares at me until I feel that I should speak. "I'm . . . I'm almost done in the front yard," I stammer. "Then I can start on your filing stuff."

Mr. Wells folds his hands on the desk. "Sam, there is no filing to be done here."

"There's not?"

He shakes his head slowly.

"Why am I here, then?"

"You're here because we need to talk," Mr. Wells says.

Even with all the candles burning and the cushy carpets underfoot, I feel a sudden chill. I turn my head to find that, behind my chair, standing between me and the closed doors, stands Dr. Sakata, arms folded. My pulse races as I turn back to Mr. Wells and square my shoulders.

"Talk? About what?"

"This." He sweeps his hands to indicate the piles of folders and CDs on his desktop. "Your history."

"I have a history?"

"So it appears." He taps a sheet of paper. "Tell me something—how many times have you been arrested?"

I practically choke. "What?"

"Are we talking one time?" he prompts. "Two? Twelve? *Twenty?*"

I finally shrug. "A few."

"A *few?*" he repeats, snapping his glasses back on and reading from a folder. "Eleven times is not 'a few.' I see here reports of vandalism . . . breaking and entering . . . shoplifting. A digital camera on one occasion. Three pairs of sneakers on another." He looks up. "And you stole an automobile?"

"It was my dad's car, and I didn't steal it," I insist. "We just borrowed it."

"And that's not everything, is it? You haven't been apprehended every time you've"—he picks his words carefully—"crossed the line."

"What do you mean?" Now this guy is freaking me out.

"This, for instance." Mr. Wells picks up a DVD and wags it at me. "This was pulled from the security system at Little John's Eat & Run. I've transferred it to my laptop. Let's take a look, shall we?"

He spins the computer around and hits a button. On the screen, in dimly lit black and white, a short figure drops from a ventilation panel in the convenience store ceiling onto the top of a dairy case. Then the figure—his face hidden by the hood of a sweatshirt—climbs down the store shelves and scurries to the deli refrigerator.

"Remember that night last May?" Mr. Wells reads from his notes. "May thirteenth, to be exact. Maybe you and some friends were hungry for a late-night snack. I mean, you did take three sandwiches from the deli case, as we'll see shortly. One for you, one for Ivy, one for Jaxon, perhaps?"

My head jerks back. "How do you know about Ivy and Jaxon?"

"I do my research, Sam."

To change the subject, I point to the screen. "Who can see this guy's face, anyway?" I scoff. "No way you can prove it's me."

"Don't be so sure." Mr. Wells hits another computer key. The on-screen image freezes and zooms in on the thief's left shoe, where the Nike swoosh is clearly visible. I stop breathing.

"Look familiar?"

"Lotta people wear Nikes," I say.

"But if you look carefully," he points out, "you can see that the swoosh is peeling off the shoe."

I lean forward and squint. There it is, plain as day.

"Exactly the way it is . . . *here.*" I look up. Mr. Wells is holding the left shoe of the pair I'd been working in all morning. The shoes I'd left on the service porch.

I bite my lip and look away.

"And that's just the tip of the iceberg, isn't it, Sam?" He drops my shoe to the floor, dusts off his hands and points to one folder after another. "I have fingerprints linking you to unsolved robberies. DNA results that place you at multiple petty crime scenes. I have pages from your school records with countless reports of fighting . . . cheating on tests . . . verbally abusing teachers . . . destroying school property."

"How . . . ? What . . . ? I mean, where did you get all this?"

"In my thirty years of foreign service, Sam, I was called upon to perform many complicated and sometimes dangerous missions. Missions that required the gathering of highly sensitive information."

A lightbulb goes off in my thick skull. "So you were, like, a *spy?*"

"Let's just say I worked in *intelligence.*"

"Isn't that like a spy?"

When he doesn't answer, I go ballistic. "You were!" I point excitedly across the desk. "You were a spy! Where? Did you ever kill anybody?"

"Must I remind you that *I'm* asking the questions here?"

"Wow! That's exactly something a spy would say!" I rub my hands together. "I always wanted to be a spy. Can you teach me?"

Ignoring my question, Mr. Wells calmly says, "Tell me about your counselor down at Family Services. Mrs. Atkinson."

"What about her?" I snap. In our sessions with Mrs. Atkinson, it always feels like she takes Dad's side. So I'm sure she hates me, but that's okay. I hate her back.

"Apparently she wants you taken from your home."

That gets my attention. "She what?"

Mr. Wells reads from a folder. "Last year, she wrote: 'Sam is a repeat offender and demonstrates no response to discipline and little chance of rehabilitation. If there are any further arrests, I recommend that it would be in the state's best interest to remove this child from his father's care.'"

The blood drains from my face. "Can she do that? Take me away from Dad?"

Mr. Wells nods gravely. Now I hate Mrs. Atkinson more than ever.

Mr. Wells wheels out from behind his desk and pulls up close to my chair. "Sam, let me lay things out for you," he says quietly. "You've gotten in a lot of trouble. You've made a lot of bad decisions. The only thing that has saved you from being shipped off into the juvenile detention system is that the cops in this town grew up with your dad, and they like him. They know he's had a hard time. He lost his job. He got divorced. He's breaking his back to save his bakery. And it doesn't help that he's got a belligerent, ungrateful son with a serious medical condition."

I look away as Mr. Wells continues. "So the Nickel Bay police want to help him out. They know you're on thin ice with Mrs. Atkinson and Family Services, so they've stopped reporting your most recent . . . *activities*."

Now he's blowing my mind. "They've really done that?"

"For almost a year now. You don't know it, but you're *this* close"—he holds up two fingers, an inch apart—"to being shipped off to juvie hall. If any one of these folders or videos were to make its way into the hands of Mrs. Atkinson, it would be buh-bye, Sam Brattle. Buh-bye, Nickel Bay."

My eyes sting, but I squeeze back any tears. "Why are you doing this to me?" I'm practically choking now. "Why are you spying on me and threatening me?"

"Because, Sam," Mr. Wells says, sitting back in his wheelchair, "I intend to blackmail you."

"You *what*?" I jump up, knocking my chair over. "Why?"

He shrugs. "It's quite simple, actually. I need your help with something, and I can't take the chance that you might say no."

We stare at each other for what feels like forever. Finally, I rattle my head to clear it. "*You* need *my* help?"

"I do."

"And I can't say no."

"I hope that you won't." He indicates the chair I'd just knocked over. "Sit back down."

As I pick up the chair and sit, Mr. Wells rolls back behind his desk. He pulls a ring of keys from his coat pocket and selects a tarnished silver one, which he uses to unlock a drawer. Out of it, he lifts a small strongbox with a combination lock.

"Please turn away," Mr. Wells says, so I look over my right shoulder. I hear the spinning of the combination dial and the creaking of the box's hinges. Then Mr. Wells speaks. "Have you ever seen one of these?"

I turn back to find him offering me a crisp, new piece of paper money. I take it and study the portrait of Benjamin Franklin.

"It's a hundred-dollar bill," I say. "So? You're rich. Big deal."

"Turn it over."

On the back, stamped in purple ink, is what looks like a carving of a bird in a circle. I squint. "Is that a phoenix?"

Mr. Wells smiles for the first time that afternoon. "Yes, a phoenix. The giant mythical bird that lives five hundred years."

"And then doesn't he build a bonfire and dive into it and burn up into ashes?" I ask. We studied Roman and Greek myths in fourth grade.

"He does. And after that, what happens to him?"

I'm supposed to be on Christmas vacation, but I feel

like I'm back in school. "He . . . what's that word? He gets *reborn* again, and then he gets to live another five hundred years. Isn't he a symbol of hope or something?"

"Very good. So sometimes you actually *do* listen in class."

I don't even react to his dig, because I suddenly gasp, realizing what I'm holding in my hand. "I've seen this phoenix before!" I exclaim. "On TV. In newspapers. Nickel Bay Nick gives away money like this every year, and it's always stamped with the same purple phoenix so everybody knows it's really Nick and not some copycat."

"Clever, isn't it?"

"It's . . . it's genius!" I stop and squint at Mr. Wells. "Wait. But Nickel Bay Nick never showed up this year. People say he's given up on this lousy town and moved away."

"That's what I've heard."

I wag the money in my hand. "So why would Nickel Bay Nick give you one of these? Doesn't he know you're loaded?"

Instead of answering, Mr. Wells pulls a four-inch cylinder of green stone from the strongbox and slides it across the desk in front of me. "Please don't touch this," he warns.

"What is it?" I ask, studying the object.

"It's called a chop," Mr. Wells explains. "In ancient China, chops were carved from rare jade—as this one is—and used by emperors and dignitaries to stamp documents with an official seal. It was their way of preventing forgeries." Very carefully Mr. Wells tilts the chop onto its side, exposing its bottom surface. I lower my face to desk level for a closer look. Carved into the pale green jade is the figure of a phoenix, stained purple. When I realize what I'm seeing, fireworks explode in my brain.

"But . . . but this . . . ," I stammer, pointing to the chop, "this is the stamp on that." I point to the hundred-dollar bill. "And that's the signature of . . . *oh my God!*"

From across the desk Mr. Wells stares at me, unblinking. It's a good thing that I went to the bathroom earlier, otherwise I'd probably wet myself.

"You're not just a spy," I whisper. *"You're Nickel Bay Nick."*

THE SURPRISE IN THE SONG

"WHERE WERE YOU THIS YEAR?"

As stupid as it sounds, that's the first question that flies out of my mouth. And I don't just ask it. I shout it.

"Why?" Mr. Wells looks startled. "Did you miss me?"

"No! I mean . . . I mean, yes!" My words can't keep up with my thoughts. "I mean, not just *me*! The whole town. Didn't you see the news? Everybody's all, 'Where's Nickel Bay Nick?' 'When's he gonna show up?' Then that turned into, 'Is he *ever* gonna show up again?' And finally it was, 'Looks like Nick's forgotten us.' It was horrible! People stopped smiling. They stopped shopping. My dad's business has been awful. Heck, everybody's business has sucked. Christmas didn't feel like Christmas." I'm really getting angry. "Don't you care about this town anymore?"

"Sam, please!" Mr. Wells gives a little laugh. "For one moment, stop and think about what it means to be Nickel Bay Nick." He polishes his glasses as he talks. "Every year for the last seven years, I have withdrawn thousands of dollars in crisp one-hundred-dollar bills from a variety of accounts I keep in banks around the country. But I never take too many from one bank. Why, do you think?"

"I dunno." I shrug.

"Use your head, Sam! Why not make one enormous withdrawal from one single bank?"

The answer hits me. "Because a big withdrawal would attract attention?"

"Exactly." He seems pleased. "Once the money arrives, I stamp each bill with the sign of the phoenix using this purple ink"—from the strongbox, he pulls a small, square bottle—"that I import from Cambodia. Nobody will ever be able to test it and trace it back to me." He replaces the ink and continues. "Then, as you know, in the weeks before Christmas, I set out to distribute my gifts. Some I send in anonymous Christmas cards, which I mail from post offices I visit across the state. Others I wrap in packages—packages without fingerprints on them, I might point out—that people find on their front porches alongside the morning paper. Or—and I think this method gets the most attention—I blend into a crowd of holiday shoppers and slip my gifts into the pockets and purses of unsuspecting citizens."

"I've seen those people on the news!" I interrupt excitedly. "They're always waving their money around and hugging each other and stuff."

"I've seen them, too. For years. But when this happened"—Mr. Wells thumps his plaster cast—"I had to face facts. I couldn't very well drive around to dozens of post offices, tiptoe onto people's porches in the dead of night or sneak around town undetected when I couldn't even walk down a flight of stairs, now could I?"

"Guess not."

"And, as much of a help as Dr. Sakata is, I couldn't ask him to perform the duties of Nickel Bay Nick. For one thing," Mr. Wells chuckles, "he's not going to blend into any crowd in this town, is he?"

I look Dr. Sakata up and down and shake my head. "No way."

"So I made the difficult decision to skip my visit this year," Mr. Wells says, "and I'm very sorry to see what that did to Nickel Bay. I never intended to cause such pain."

"Wait a second," I say, suddenly suspicious. "Why are you telling me this? All these years, you haven't told a soul, and now suddenly you're spilling your guts to me?" A horrible thought occurs to me. "Are you going to have to kill me now?"

Mr. Wells throws back his head and roars with laughter. "Nobody's killing anybody, Sam," he says. "You obviously have the wrong impression of my past. I never jumped from a burning plane or crashed a speeding car or disarmed a ticking bomb. But all my years of training, all the tricks I acquired and all the schemes I hatched during my career, those come in very handy when I assume the role of Nickel Bay Nick." He lowers his voice when he asks, "Can you understand, Sam, how challenging it is to do what I've done for as long as I've done it and still remain a mystery?"

"It's tough, huh?"

"Nearly impossible. Being Nickel Bay Nick requires a quick and devious mind. It requires the ability to move in the shadows, never attracting attention or leaving clues behind. In short, it requires the skills of a thief."

"So? I still don't get it." I shrug. "Why am I here?"

"You are here, Sam"—he looks me in the eye—"because you already *are* a thief."

I stare back until I realize what Mr. Wells just said. Then my heart starts thumping like a jackhammer. "Wait a sec. Are you saying . . . ?"

"I am."

I gasp. "You want me to be Nickel Bay Nick?"

"Think of yourself as my understudy."

"Whoa, whoa, whoa!" I wave my hands. "That's crazy!"

"I've seen your police files, Sam," Mr. Wells says. "You want to talk about crazy?"

"But, I'm . . . I'm just a kid," I stutter. "And besides, it's too late now! Christmas is over."

"Far from it," Mr. Wells says. "Have you ever heard the carol about the twelve days of Christmas?" He starts to sing, "*On the first day of Christmas, my true love gave to me . . .*"

"Yeah, yeah, I know," I interrupt and sing the rest of the line. "*A cartridge in a pear tree.*"

"A what? A *cartridge?*" Mr. Wells sputters in surprise. "It's 'a partridge in a pear tree.' A *partridge,* Sam, not a *cartridge.* It's a bird, not a bullet."

"Hmm," I grunt. "So all this time, I've been singing it wrong."

Mr. Wells holds up a calendar that's open to the month of December. "Take a look at this," he says as he runs a finger over the first three weeks. "Nowadays we celebrate Christmas *before* December twenty-fifth. But hundreds of years ago, people actually began their festivities at sunset on Christmas Day, which makes today"—he taps December 26 on the page—"the *first day of Christmas.* Like in the song. Celebrations would then continue for the last six days of the old year and"—he flips the calendar page— "the first six days of the new one. Twelve days of Christmas, ending at sunset on the sixth of January."

"January sixth?" I scrunch up my face. "That's the last day of my Christmas vacation."

"Good. Then you're available to work for me."

I don't like the way this guy is taking over my life. "What if don't want to do this?" I ask. "What if I don't want to be your understudy Nick?"

Mr. Wells sits back and studies me. "I thought that you'd be intrigued by a secret mission. I thought you'd jump at the opportunity to bring a little Christmas cheer back to Nickel Bay and help your father's business in the bargain. But maybe I was wrong. So, if that doesn't persuade you, then please remember this." With one bony finger, Mr. Wells points at me. "You vandalized my property," he growls. "Either you work off your debt, or your father can pay me for the damage you caused."

I have to admit this guy is creeping me out. "And what do you expect me to do, exactly?"

"You'll receive your assignments as we go along." He picks up a manila envelope and extends it across the desk. "This evening, you will go home and study the pages in here. Then you'll bring that back when you report for work tomorrow." As I take the envelope, he adds, "The contents are for your eyes only."

That sounds like something a spy would say, and despite my annoyance, a prickle of excitement runs down my spine.

"Should your father ask," he says, "tell him that my storage rooms and files are in far worse shape than I originally thought and that you'll be working every day for me until your vacation ends." He looks down at his calendar and announces, "Tomorrow morning, be here at eight thirty sharp." He looks up. "Do you have a wristwatch? We'll need to coordinate timetables as we go along."

"Yeah, I have a wristwatch," I say with more than a little attitude. "A Rolex, actually."

Mr. Wells's eyebrows arch. "A Rolex? What's a boy your age doing with an expensive timepiece like that?"

"My mom sent it to me after I got my new heart," I answer. "After she forgot that she'd promised to visit me in the hospital and then never showed up."

"Your mother never visited you?"

"She had things to do. Out of town," I snap, feeling an unexpected heat rising up my neck. "Why's that your business?"

Mr. Wells is silent for a moment, then he puts his glasses back on.

"It's not." He waves a hand impatiently. "That's all for now."

With one eye on Hoko, I stand, clamp the manila envelope under my arm and turn for the door that I came in through.

"Not that way!" Mr. Wells spits out. I turn back to him. "From now on, you will use the back door," he says, pointing to a hallway leading off the far corner of the living room. "I can't risk having a neighbor notice your comings and goings. Are we clear?"

"Crystal," I mutter.

Dr. Sakata steps forward holding not only my shoes but my jacket and gloves as well. As I put them on, Mr. Wells says, "At the northeast corner of my backyard, you'll find a security gate. The combination is oh-one-oh-five. Can you remember that, or should I write it down?"

"Oh-one-oh-five," I repeat. "I'm not an idiot."

Mr. Wells pretends he doesn't hear me. "The gate is engineered to close slowly, so do not walk away until it shuts firmly. I don't want anyone sneaking onto my property. You will then find yourself in the alley that runs the length of the block and wraps around behind your place. You know the alley I mean?"

Slipping into my shoes, I grumble, "Yeah, I know it." I straighten up and glare at him one final time. "You know, I bet there are a few reporters in Nickel Bay who'd pay to hear everything you told me here today."

He tilts his head. "What are you saying?"

"I'm just saying it might be worth it to toss a couple of those Benjamins my way. To keep me quiet."

"Are you now trying to blackmail *me*, Sam?" Mr. Wells spreads his arms over the files and videos on his desktop. "Because, you know, two can play that game. In which case"—he gives a little wave—"buh-bye, Sam Brattle. Buh-bye, Nickel Bay."

I jut my chin, determined not to let him see that he's won this round.

"Sam," says Mr. Wells, "anyone ever tell you that you've got a cold heart?"

"So what?" I sneer on my way out. "It's not mine."

THE HISTORY OF A MYSTERY

Early evening shadows have already begun to swallow up the winter-bare flower beds and rock gardens when I step into Mr. Wells's backyard. You could never tell by looking at the front of the house, but it's the size of a baseball infield. Flagstone paths wind every which way and disappear into groves of naked trees. In a far corner of the yard I find the gate he's told me to use, and I punch in the code. Oh-one-oh-five. The gate pops open, and once I exit into the alley, I watch it hiss shut until—*click!*—it locks into place.

Since the city's plows never turn down these alleys, the snow here is slushy and deep. Potholes and puddles make my route home an obstacle course. By the time I slop around to the back of my house and squeeze through a couple of rotting boards on the back fence, my shoes and pant legs are soaked.

"How was your first day of work?" is the first thing Dad asks when I call him at work.

"Fine," is all I say.

"Did Mr. Wells feed you?"

"Soup and stuff, yeah. When're you coming home?"

"Couple hours. Why? You hungry?"

"Nah. I can wait."

I hang up. Now that I know I've got the place to myself, I carefully open the envelope that Mr. Wells has given me and empty the contents onto the kitchen table. Out slide dozens of clippings about Nickel Bay Nick from papers like the *New York Times* and the *London Observer*. I find pages out of *Time* and *People* magazines, and articles in a lot of foreign languages. I always knew he was famous in Nickel Bay, but I never realized that the story of Nick had spread all over the world. When I remember that I'll be playing that part this year, my mouth goes dry.

I learn a lot of things I didn't know, or hardly remembered. Like the fact that everybody calls his gifts Nickel Bay Bucks. Or Nickel Bay Bens, since Ben Franklin's picture is on the front of the hundred-dollar bill. There are plenty of stories about grateful people whose lives were changed or whose prayers were answered when they received a Ben. One man told how Nickel Bay Nick's gift bought enough heating oil to keep his family from freezing in December. An elderly couple said they were able to pay their rent instead of being forced into a homeless shelter on Christmas Eve.

Just like Mr. Wells predicted they would, detectives from all over have dusted his gift wrappings and Christmas cards for fingerprints. They've analyzed the purple ink and tried to trace the serial numbers on the money, hoping to "unmask" Nickel Bay Nick.

They got nothing.

By the time I work my way through the piles of clippings, I'm impressed and intimidated. Nickel Bay Nick—I mean, Mr. Wells—has touched lives and saved Christmas for a lot of people in our town. He's given unselfishly, never expecting any kind of thanks. And he's never been caught.

How could a man like that be such a grouch? And a *blackmailer*?

I don't realize how much time has passed until the sound of Dad's car sends me into a panic. Scooping up the clippings, I race into my bedroom, where I stuff everything back into the brown envelope and slide it under my mattress.

"What's going on?" Dad's suddenly behind me, standing in the doorway that has no door.

Down on my knees at my bedside, I turn to Dad with all the innocence I can muster and fold my hands. "Just saying a few prayers."

Dad's eyes bug out in surprise. "Since when do you pray?"

"Since I thought we might need some help."

"I can't disagree," Dad grunts. He starts to leave, but

he turns back to say, "Could you maybe put in a plug for the bakery while you're at it?"

Dad rarely lets on when something's bothering him, so I figure things must really be serious. "Let me see what I can do," I say, and when he goes, I actually do mutter a quick prayer. In case someone's listening.

Later, Dad microwaves a couple of frozen mini-pizzas. "I asked around about our neighbor," he says as we eat. "Nobody's got any idea where this Mr. Wells is from. What he does. What he *did*. Amazing, isn't it?"

I shrug. "If you say so."

"A guy lives in one place for this long, you'd think he'd drop a clue or two." Dad leans in. "Did he tell you any more about what he did in the Foreign Service?"

"I was in the yard all day," I lie, holding up my hands. "Nearly froze my fingers off."

When Dad's wristwatch buzzes and he clicks off the alarm, we say, "Seven thirty," in unison before I swallow my pill.

Just then Jaxon's ring tone rattles my cell phone. While Dad frowns, I scoot into my bedroom, flip open the phone and mutter, "What's up, man?"

"Sam the Man!" Jaxon shouts. He's got about a dozen funny names for me. "Say hello to Ivy."

"Hey, Sam." It's Ivy. Jaxon has us on a three-way call.

"Oh, Ivy. How's it . . . how's it going?" I stammer. "I mean, how was your Christmas?" Even though we've

68

been hanging out for a while now, I still sometimes get tongue-tied around her.

"You kids can talk later," Jaxon says before Ivy can answer. "We're calling you, Samster, to ask if you wanna hang with us tomorrow. Me and Ivy are gonna check out some of the after-Christmas sales." He giggles his crazy giggle. "If you know what I mean."

I know what he means.

"So. You wanna go . . . *shopping?*" Jaxon taunts.

"Can't," I reply. "My dad made me get a job."

"A job?" That's Ivy asking. "You mean at the bakery?"

"Nah. I'm working for this old neighbor guy down the street. Cleaning out his basement and stuff."

"Well, tell your neighbor to shove it," Jaxon orders. "And while you're at it, tell your dad to shove it."

I laugh just as a shadow falls across my desk. "Gotta go," I whisper into the phone, and snap it shut.

"What's he want?"

"The usual." I shrug. "He asked if I wanted to hang out. Stuff like that."

"I wish you had a few friends your own age," Dad says.

"And I wish I was a rock star."

Lying awake later, I slip a hand under my mattress to make sure Mr. Wells's papers are still there. With the history of Nickel Bay Nick at my fingertips, my pulse quickens at the thought that tomorrow, I'm going to become a part of that legacy.

THE MONKEY AROUND MY NECK
December 27

The next morning, Dad only hangs around long enough to make sure I take my seven-thirty pill, and then he leaves for work. Once I'm sure he's gone, I drag the kitchen step stool into Dad's bedroom closet and pull a velvet box from the back of his top shelf. In it he keeps a pair of gold cuff links, his high school class ring and my Rolex wristwatch.

I set the time according to the clock over the stove—7:51. Very carefully, I wind the watch, hold it to my ear, and when I hear it ticking, my heart skips a beat. I strap it on, and even though the watchband hangs loosely on my wrist because my bones are so small, the Rolex looks awesome.

I've never felt so mysterious in my life.

At 8:20, I tuck Mr. Wells's brown envelope under my sweater, pull on my new gloves and zip up my winter coat. At the bottom of the stairs that go from our apartment down to the back of the garage we live over, I pause to scope out my surroundings.

All clear on the left?

Check.

All clear on the right?

Check.

I'm getting good at this spy stuff.

I slide through our back fence and head down the alley to my first assignment as Nickel Bay Nick.

Oh-one-oh-five, and I'm in Mr. Wells's backyard. A quick dash and I'm up on the porch, punching the bell. Inside, Hoko answers the chimes with a racket of his own, and then Dr. Sakata is suddenly filling the doorway. As he lets me in, he glances quickly around the backyard to make sure nobody's seen us.

From another part of the house comes the sound of Hoko's nails clicking as he races down stairs and gallops across wood floors, snarling and woofing on his way.

"He's coming!" I yell to Dr. Sakata. "Do something!"

Maybe he can't understand my words, but Dr. Sakata can't miss the panic in my voice. He shouts, "Hoko! KO-ra!" and in the next room, the clicking stops as Hoko hits the brakes. Like a car skidding on a wet street, Hoko slides around the corner of the doorway and slams into Dr. Sakata's leg. He looks up at me and, with his black tongue, he licks his chops as if to say, *Next time, you're mine.*

Dr. Sakata holds out a hand, and I pass him my coat and gloves. When he points to my shoes, I slip them off as well.

"We've got our own special sign language going, huh?" I ask, but he doesn't even blink before he's striding down another hallway. I rush to keep up with him, slipping on the waxed wood in my socks as Hoko follows close behind. We turn into a whole new wing of the house, one that I'd never have guessed was here, and we pass a few closed doors before we enter what appears to be another office.

Unlike the freaky living room, this place looks as modern as a command center at the Pentagon. At a steel table that runs down the middle of the room, Mr. Wells, surrounded by piles of papers and folders, is thumbing through a stack of file cards. I quickly look around for any clues to his life—family photographs, framed diplomas, stuff like that. The wall behind Mr. Wells is covered up by a map of the world, and gray file cabinets line the walls to the right and the left. Up high, around the perimeter of the room, twenty-four small clocks are arranged to show the time of day in cities all over the globe. But that's about it, as far as decorations go.

I pull the brown envelope from under my sweater and lay it on the desk in front of Mr. Wells. "Brought your stuff back."

Without looking up, he glances at his wristwatch. "What time have you got?"

I check. "Eight thirty-one."

"Actually, it's eight thirty-five. You're late."

He hasn't even said good morning yet, and already he's giving me grief! "But I've got a Rolex," I protest. "How can it be wrong?"

"I'm going to guess that the clock by which you set your wristwatch is incorrect," he answers. "Be sure to reset *that* clock this evening." He rolls out from behind the desk and indicates the wall behind me. "Let's get started, shall we?"

I quickly reset my wristwatch and then turn around to face a huge cork bulletin board. In the center of it is a street map of Nickel Bay that's stuck all over with green, red and white pins. A banner across the top of the corkboard reads OPERATION CHRISTMAS RESCUE.

"*Operation Christmas Rescue*? Is that what we're calling this?" I ask, and, yeah, maybe I sound a little sarcastic when I do.

Mr. Wells ignores my question and instead asks one of his own. "Did you read the pages I sent home with you last evening?"

"Yeah."

"Did you learn anything that you didn't know before?"

"I didn't know Nickel Bay Nick is world-famous."

He nods. "Anything else?"

I squint in concentration. "Oh! He makes three visits every year, always four days apart, and the last one's always on Christmas Eve. Until this year."

For the first time ever, Mr. Wells looks at me with an expression that is almost admiring.

"What?" I ask.

"That's correct," he murmurs before continuing. "Now, it's too late to send greeting cards or secretly deliver Christmas gifts, so we're going to have to get creative if we hope to deliver the usual forty-five Nickel Bay Bucks in time."

Pulling on a pair of white cotton gloves, he unzips a small canvas bag in his lap, pulls out a stack of crisp green bills and runs a thumb across the edges. "Four thousand five hundred dollars," he announces as they flip past. When I feel the breeze on my face, I gulp. I've never seen so much money. Not up close.

Mr. Wells replaces the cash and removes his gloves before turning back to the map. "In keeping with tradition, between now and January sixth, Nickel Bay Nick will perform three missions." From a pocket he pulls what looks like a silver lipstick tube. When he twists it, a long metal wand telescopes out. "As you can see," he says, tapping on the bulletin board with the pointer, "I've assigned a color to each mission—red, green and white."

"Christmas colors," I note.

"Exactly," he says crisply. "Today, we will commence with the Red Mission."

I stand on tiptoe to study the cluster of red-headed pins stuck into the map. "Looks like they're all downtown."

"Very observant," he says as he spins his chair and

returns to the steel table. He points at the empty chair across from him. "You may sit."

Once I do, he slides a writing tablet and a pen over to me. Down the left-hand margin of the tablet he has written FIRST, SECOND, THIRD, FOURTH. He holds up a wall calendar, and with his pointer, he whacks each day as he mentions it.

"Yesterday, as you will remember, was the first day of Christmas."

Whack! He hits December 26.

"Today is the second day . . ."

Whack!

". . . which I will use to explain the Red Mission. To-morrow, on the third day of Christmas . . ."

Whack!

". . . we will lay the groundwork and make all preparations for you to make the first distribution on December twenty-ninth . . ."

Whack! Whack!

". . . the fourth day of Christmas. Nickel Bay Nick's return. Any questions so far?"

"Yeah," I say, wrinkling my nose. "Could you please stop smacking that stick around? It's really irritating, and it's kind of insulting."

My bluntness seems to catch him by surprise.

"Oh." He collapses the pointer down into its tube.

"And one more thing?" I figure that while I have him off balance, why not shoot for the moon? "Can you please not talk to me like I'm a subhuman life-form? I may be a problem kid, but I'm not a stupid one."

Mr. Wells looks at me a long time before he twists his neck as if he were working out a crick.

"Fair enough, Sam," he says. "Let's begin."

The morning flies by. At noon, the desktop between us is covered with fifteen advertisements that Mr. Wells and I have clipped from the sales pages of the *Nickel Bay News*. Each ad is from a different store, and each one is for a different, everyday product that's been drastically marked down for post-Christmas clearance. Toothpaste. Shoe polish. A pack of playing cards. Stuff like that.

"According to my research," Mr. Wells explains, "these items are among the most likely to be purchased when they go on sale."

We've labeled each ad with Post-its numbered from one to fifteen, and on a map of Nickel Bay, we've assigned each number to a store where that ad's product is sold.

"So talk me through this," Mr. Wells says. "Tomorrow, how will you start?"

I push back my sleeves and point to a spot on the map. "I guess I'm going to pick up item number one—the box of women's hair dye—in store number one, which is . . . Colodner's Drugstore."

"Correct."

I look up. "Can I ask you something?"

He nods.

"Is there any particular reason I'm starting at Colodner's?"

Mr. Wells looks puzzled. "Why would there be?"

If he doesn't know, I'm not going to tell him, but I once got arrested at Colodner's. Until Mr. Colodner wised up and put in surveillance cameras, his store was where Jaxon and Ivy and I used to "shop" for all of our back-to-school supplies. Then one day, after slipping a three-ring binder under my jacket, I turned around to find Mr. Colodner with a cop at his side. I haven't been back since.

I fake a smile for Mr. Wells. "Nope, no reason," I say quickly as I walk my fingers across the map. "Then, for item number two—a package of four double-A batteries— I cross the street to store number two. Hopkins Hardware."

"Precisely," Mr. Wells declares. "And if you simply follow the sequence of numbers on the map, you'll never waste a step. Once you're done with your route, what do you do with the items you've collected?"

"I bring them all back here, and then, I guess, we stick Nickel Bay Bucks into them?"

"So far, so good. You'll need this." He slides a white letter-size envelope across the table to me. I open it to find a stack of paper money—ones, fives and tens—and rolling around at the bottom of the envelope is a bunch of coins.

"What's this for?"

"That is exactly as much cash as you will need to purchase all these items tomorrow."

"Wait a second!" I blurt out. "I'm supposed to *buy* all these things?"

"How did you think you were going to get them out of the stores?" Mr. Wells asks.

"I thought I was going to . . . y'know . . ." I pretend to pick up an imaginary object and slip it into my pocket.

Mr. Wells wrinkles his brow. "You think I'd ask you to steal?"

"Well, you're the one who said you needed a thief!"

"But I'm not going to have you shoplift on Day One of the Red Mission!" he insists. "What if you got caught? Operation Christmas Rescue would have to be scrapped."

I sulk for a moment. "Well, what do you need a thief for, then?"

"Ah." Mr. Wells holds up a finger. "I need a thief for the day *after* tomorrow."

"December twenty-ninth?"

"Exactly. The fourth day of Christmas is when you will retrace the route we have plotted today and return everything where you got it. Same exact shelf. Same exact position. *That* will take the cunning and concentration of a thief. Are you up to the challenge?"

I scowl and shrug. "We'll see, won't we?"

Mr. Wells keeps ignoring all the attitude I'm tossing his way, and we work through the rest of my assignment in agonizing detail.

At one o'clock—according to my Rolex—Dr. Sakata serves us each a bowl of really good tomato soup and a chicken salad sandwich. He and Mr. Wells talk for a few minutes in that language I don't understand, and then Dr. Sakata leaves us to eat in silence. Looking down the table at the mounds of notes and cards and clippings, I suddenly feel overwhelmed by the task ahead of me.

"It's not the job you imagined, is it?" Mr. Wells asks, and I look across to find him studying me.

"Hardly," I say. "I thought that, y'know, being Nickel Bay Nick, all I'd have to do is run around town, giving away money. But this . . ." I jerk a thumb at the clutter around us. "All this mapping and memorizing, this is worse than being in school."

"Keeping a secret is very tough work," he says, and returns to his lunch.

I'm getting so warm from the soup that I pull my sweater over my head and toss it aside. Mr. Wells looks at me, and his eyes narrow.

"That object around your neck," he says, pointing to his own throat. "I haven't noticed it before."

"Oh, this?" I rub the little stone carving between two fingers. "Maybe cuz it's always been under my sweater."

"Is there a story behind it?" he asks.

"Yeah," I say. "It's a long one, though."

Mr. Wells spreads his arms wide. "I've got all the time in the world."

"Well, okay." I finish my last spoonful of soup and take a deep breath.

"D'you ever hear about the big fire that burned down the Nickel Bay Furniture Works?"

"I heard it was horrible," Mr. Wells says. "But I also heard that there was one particularly heroic firefighter. Saved a dozen lives, if I remember correctly?"

I nod. "That was my dad."

Mr. Wells blinks in surprise. "Dwight? Really?"

"Yeah. Anyway, because of that, he got written up in papers all over the country. He even got interviewed on the *Today* show. I was three and a half at the time, so I really had no idea how famous my dad was, if only for a few weeks.

"Then the bad news started. After the factory closed, people started leaving town to look for other work and more businesses shut down. So the town of Nickel Bay cut the fire department's budget, and Dad lost his job. Six months later, when the doctors found out I'd need a new heart, the same reporters who wrote about Dad's bravery wrote stories about me. Y'know, things like, 'Hero's Child Needs Heart!'

"When I finally had the operation, it got reported everywhere. Mom even came back to see me and gave a few interviews. But she had a job singing on a riverboat outside St. Louis, so she had to leave before she could visit the hospital."

"Is that when she sent you the Rolex?" Mr. Wells asks.

"Uh-huh."

"Even though you were too small to wear it and too young to tell time?"

"It was her way of apologizing, okay?" I say, feeling a little defensive.

Mr. Wells holds up his hands. "Whatever you say."

"Anyway," I continue, "my hospital room was flooded with all kinds of *heart* gifts . . . heart-shaped candies and heart-shaped balloons and pajamas and T-shirts with hearts on them, and—"

"Okay." Mr. Wells smiles. "I get the idea."

"Dad donated most of that stuff to other kids in the hospital, and one of the only gifts he kept was a wooden box with this inside it, hanging from a leather cord." I squint at my pendant. "There was no card, Dad said, so we never knew who it came from. Or what it was supposed to be. We thought it looked like a monkey, but we were never sure. Dad says I used to swing it back and forth and stare at it for hours, but then I got over it and stuck it in my sock drawer.

"I didn't think about it again until the day my third-grade class took a field trip to an art museum upstate. I happened to look into a room we were marching past, and I saw a stone statue as tall as me, exactly like my carving. I got yelled at for breaking out of line, but I had to get a closer look. And before my teacher dragged me off, I read the card next to the statue that told how Hanuman was a god of India with the head of a monkey and the body of a man."

"Oh, that's Hanuman, is it?" Mr. Wells asks, leaning forward for a closer look. "Hmm. So it is."

"You know about Hanuman?"

"Of course. I once lived in India. He's very popular there."

"Anyway, when I got home from the museum that day, I pulled this pendant out and told Dad how I'd learned that Hanuman is a monkey and a man. 'Do you believe it?' I said. 'He's two creatures in one body. Like me!'"

"Hold on," Mr. Wells says. "You thought of yourself as two creatures in one body?"

"I still do."

"Explain, please."

"Well, after my operation, nobody would ever answer when I asked where my heart came from, so I never knew anything about this . . . thing I've got living inside me," I say, thumping my chest. "Over time, my imagination filled in the blanks, and I started having these awesome dreams. Like, there was one where I had the strength of ten men because I'd received the heart of a lion. In another one, I got the heart of a dolphin, so I could swim under any ocean on the planet.

"I told Dad that if anyone would understand what it's like to be two creatures in one body, it would be Hanuman. So that day, he tied this around my neck. And I've been wearing it ever since."

"You know, millions of people in India wear carvings like yours in the belief that Hanuman will protect them," Mr. Wells says. "Like a guardian angel."

"And does he?" I ask. "Protect them?"

"You fell from my roof onto my front lawn, and yet here you are." He shrugs. "What do you think?"

After Dr. Sakata clears our lunch plates, we spend the afternoon rehearsing. First, Mr. Wells makes me memorize the exact order of the stores I'll visit tomorrow as well as the item I'm supposed to buy in each one. Then I have to walk around the room, stopping every few feet, pretending to make a purchase and announcing stuff like, "At Veckens Stationery, I buy the box of twenty letter-size white envelopes on sale for two dollars and nineteen cents." Boring, right?

"Why can't I just take my notes with me?" I ask after the third rehearsal.

"Because you don't want to . . . what?"

His words come back to me. "Attract attention," I mumble.

"Exactly!" he practically shouts. "You want to be a spy? Think like one."

Before I can give him any grief, he plunges ahead. "Now, let's discuss your wardrobe. Everything you wear," he warns me, "must be in drab colors. Nothing flashy. Nothing that anyone might notice."

He cautions me to avoid salesclerks who know me. "Most of these stores still have temporary holiday cashiers, so be sure to buy your items at their registers. And *do not make conversation!*" He pounds a fist. "I don't want anyone to have any memory of you."

"Okay, okay, I get it."

"And in every store that you enter, be sure to note the location of surveillance cameras."

"Why? I'm not doing anything illegal."

"No, you're not. But when you reshelve the merchandise the next day, you want to avoid being caught on video. You know how that can come back to haunt you."

I curl my top lip. "Ha-ha. Very funny."

The hands of my Rolex are creeping toward four o'clock when I collapse in a chair and ask wearily, "Are we done for today?"

"Hardly!" Mr. Wells exclaims, and he buzzes the desk intercom. Dr. Sakata enters and takes up his position behind Mr. Wells's chair.

"Of the three missions in Operation Christmas Rescue," Mr. Wells says, "the one that concerns me the most is the last one. The White Mission. It's also the most"—he waves a hand, trying to find the word—"*popular.*"

"Which one's the White Mission?"

"That's the one where Nick maneuvers through a holiday crowd and slips money into the pockets and purses of unsuspecting shoppers."

"Yeah, that always gets a lot of buzz," I remember. "So, why are we talking about it now?"

"Because it requires a skill that I'm afraid you're lacking at present."

I sit up, insulted. "And what's that?"

"I don't believe you know the first thing about being a pickpocket." He points toward my police files on his desk. "There's nothing in your record of arrests to indicate that you've ever cultivated that talent."

He's right. Jaxon's always trying to get me to try it—to walk into a crowd and walk out with someone's wallet or cell phone. But I never have.

"Just because I haven't doesn't mean I can't," I say, cocky.

"I'm curious," Mr. Wells says. "You obviously have no problem with taking things that aren't yours. Why do you draw the line at pickpocketing?"

"I don't know." I shrug. "Maybe cuz I don't like to see the people I'm taking things from."

"Well, well, well." Mr. Wells nods. "Perhaps Sam has a conscience after all." My cheeks flush with anger, but before I can explode, Mr. Wells moves on. "You need training, because once you acquire the skills to be a pickpocket, you can be a put-pocket."

"A what?"

"A *put-pocket*. Instead of taking something *from* someone—we'll call that person your 'mark'—you can slip
something *to* them." He jerks a thumb over his shoulder.
"You'll start your training with Dr. Sakata here."

Hearing his name, the big guy moves out from behind
the desk and bows slightly to me.

"Fine, let's do this." I stand and stretch. "How hard
could it be?"

Well, it turns out it's not hard.

It's impossible.

Mr. Wells puts us through drills where Dr. Sakata pretends to be an ordinary guy on the street. I'm supposed
to casually pass by and slip my hand in a pocket. Every
time I do, he nails me.

From the sidelines, Mr. Wells makes suggestions:

"Make believe you've stumbled into him."

"Pretend you're brushing a spider off his jacket."

"Divert his attention somehow!"

So I try to distract Dr. Sakata by pointing to the ceiling and crying, "Look! A burning building!" Maybe because he doesn't speak English, he never takes the bait.
At the end of an hour, it's clear I've failed my first lesson
in pickpocketing. Or put-pocketing.

Whatever.

"You see why I'm starting your lessons early?" Mr.
Wells asks.

"I just need a little more practice," I insist.

"You just need a lot more practice."

Since I can't disagree, I don't reply. Mr. Wells turns his wheelchair and asks, "What time do you start shopping tomorrow morning?"

"When the stores open at nine," I answer without thinking.

"And your first visit is . . . ?"

"Colodner's. Where I will buy one box of women's chestnut-brown hair dye, on sale for three dollars and ninety-five cents. That's including tax." I cock my head defiantly. "You want my whole schedule?"

"I know your whole schedule," he snaps back, "and as long as you follow our plan, you'll be done in ninety minutes. Accounting for travel time, I'll expect you at my back door no later than eleven." He wheels out of the room, calling over one shoulder, "And please . . . don't disappoint me on your first day."

Just as I'm about to make a rude gesture toward the departing wheelchair, Dr. Sakata steps into the doorway, holding my coat and shoes. I can't be sure if the big doctor can understand the language of rude gestures, but I'm not taking any chances.

THE WISHES IN THE JAR

December 27–28

I wait long enough to make sure Mr. Wells's back gate hisses closed, and then I start down the alley, stopping every few steps to practice buying an item at each of the fifteen stores on my memorized list. Halfway through my route, I'm standing under a stuttering streetlight when I hear the idling of a motor. Down the alley I can see Crummer Sikes watching me from behind the wheel of his white van, the one that says NICKEL BAY DEPARTMENT OF ANIMAL CONTROL across the side. People joke that the only animal in Nickel Bay that needs controlling is Crummer Sikes.

He went to high school with my dad, but Crummer dropped out before graduating when drug-sniffing police dogs made a beeline for his locker during a random inspection. These days Crummer wears his greasy hair in a long braid down his back and always smells like a spilled beer and the herbal cigarettes he smokes. But somehow, despite all the cutbacks in city services in Nickel Bay, he's managed to hang on to his job as the town's dog-catcher.

"Hey, Crummer," I call.

"Sam." He nods and rolls up alongside me in his van. "Who are you talkin' to?"

"Me?" I realize Crummer caught me rehearsing the Red Mission, so I do what I do best. I lie. "I'm talking to the voices inside my head. But, then, you know all about talking to the voices inside your head, right, Crummer?"

He sneers. "You oughta have some respect for your elders." He flicks the smoldering butt of his stinky herbal cigarette in my direction, and I jump out of its way. Crummer laughs like a Halloween witch, hits the gas and peels out, splattering me with snowy mud and pebbles.

My cell phone rings, and I check my wristwatch. Seven thirty.

"I'm taking my pill, okay?" I answer.

"Where are you?" Dad asks.

"Heading home. What about you?"

"Three minutes away."

I suddenly freeze. Staring down at my Rolex, I try to remember whether I put Dad's velvet box back in his closet after pulling the watch out earlier.

"See ya there!" I shout, snapping my phone closed and racing down the alley like a cat on fire. On my way, I un-strap my watch and shove it into my pants.

As I feared, I hadn't replaced Dad's velvet box, and I

hadn't returned the kitchen stepladder to its place next to the washing machine. I do both in record time, and I'm still panting when Dad walks through the front door.

"Are you okay?" he asks, leaning close. "You're sweating like a racehorse."

"I'm fine, I'm fine," I insist and push past him, terrified that he'll hear the *tick tick tick* of the Rolex in my pants.

"Wait." He follows, trying to put a palm on my forehead. "Are you running a fever?"

"No!"

"Sam, you're very warm!"

"That's . . . because . . ." I stall until an idea hits. "*Because* Mr. Wells gave me a cup of hot cocoa before I left, and *whew*!" I fan my face with both hands. "Hot cocoa, y'know?"

"So take your jacket off," Dad suggests.

"Great idea!"

And that *would* be a great idea if Mr. Wells's envelope of cash wasn't under my jacket, sticking out of my waistband. So I rub my arms vigorously and do my best to shiver. "But am I the only one in here who's freezing?"

"Do I need to take your temperature?" Dad asks.

"I'll do it!" I dash past him into the bathroom and close the door. Three minutes later, I shout out, "Ninety-eight-point-six!" and that puts an end to that conversation.

I'm sprawled on the couch, eating take-out fried chicken and watching TV, when Dad leaves to meet Lisa for dinner. As soon as I hear his car pull away, I dump my plate in the kitchen sink and start making preparations.

From my pants pocket I retrieve the wristwatch, and once I use it to reset the correct time on the oven clock, I slide it between my mattress and box spring.

Digging through my closets and drawers, I find the dullest colored sweater, scarf and knit cap that I own.

Then I count out Mr. Wells's cash—$54.17—and zip it into one of the many pouches in my backpack.

What I'm doing tomorrow is totally legal, and yet my pulse is pounding like I'm about to crack Fort Knox.

At breakfast the next morning, Dad's looking over his monthly bills. "Where does the time go?" he worries, running his hand through his hair. "It's already December twenty-eighth."

Without thinking, I blurt, "The third day of Christmas."

Dad looks up. "The what?"

I stop breathing. "Huh?"

"You said 'the third' what?"

"You think I said 'third'? I didn't say 'third.' Wow. Your ears need cleaning." I laugh too loudly, thinking fast. "I said . . . 'the *worst*.' The worst kind of Christmas."

"Ain't that the truth?" Dad agrees, and goes back to writing his checks.

Waiting for the stores to open is agony. I get dressed, check my backpack, wind my wristwatch, pocket my cell phone, pull on my gloves . . . and it's not even eight o'clock yet. Mr. Wells warned me about getting downtown too early and attracting attention, so I sit on the edge of the bed and try to slow down my breath. At 8:40, I finally leave the house and head for the first stop on my buying tour.

I stroll through the doors of Colodner's Drugstore on First Avenue at 9:02. Luckily, I don't run into Mr. Colodner on my way to the hair care aisle, where I quickly locate a box of women's chestnut-brown hair dye. At the cash register I keep my head bowed and count out $3.95 for a tall, skinny lady clerk I've never seen before.

"So," she says brightly, "how was your Christmas?"

I wince and whimper, "Can we please not talk about it?" as I slide the bills and coins across to her.

She doesn't ask any more questions.

In my haste to get out of there, I grab the plastic shopping bag but don't bother to zip it into my backpack. As I exit the store, I hear the crackling static of a bullhorn, and an amplified voice behind me bellows, "HOLD IT RIGHT THERE!" I gasp and whip around to find Jaxon and Ivy on a bus stop bench. Jaxon's hands are cupped around his mouth, and when he shouts, "WHAT'S IN THE BAG, YOUNG MAN?" he sounds exactly like a police car loudspeaker.

I guess I must look pretty shocked, because Jaxon doubles over with laughter. "I wish I had a picture of your face, Sammy-boy!" he howls.

"Ha-ha, very funny." I try to sound casual, but my pulse is pounding.

"Hey, Sam," Ivy says, tossing back her long blond hair.

"Hey, Ivy," I answer timidly.

Jaxon recovers enough to say, "Hey! I thought you had to work for that old man today."

"I . . . I do," I answer nervously, and I wave the plastic bag as proof. "He's got me doing his shopping."

"What'd ya buy?" Ivy asks.

"Oh . . . uh . . . you know," I stammer. "Stuff."

"What kind of stuff?" Jaxon demands, and before I can react, he grabs the bag from my hand and yanks out the . . .

"*Hair dye?!*" He looks up. "What's your boss gonna do with hair dye?"

My jaw flaps. "I . . . I just buy what I'm told."

I reach for the box, but Jaxon pulls it back and reads the label.

"*Women's* hair dye? Your boss is twisted, man."

"That's not so twisted," Ivy says, snatching it from Jaxon's hands. "Lots of guys color their hair nowadays."

"Ivy's right," I announce, slipping up beside her and reaching for the box.

"Not so fast," she says, holding it up, out of my reach. "I'm reading the warning."

"The *warning*?" I blink.

"Yeah. It's so interesting, all the chemicals they warn

93

you about these days. And hair dye's full of chemicals, so there's always a warning."

"I got a warning for the Samster," Jaxon says, grabbing the dye from Ivy. "Try to get it back!"

"C'mon, Jaxon!" I lunge at him, but he jumps off the curb, laughing as he dashes into traffic. Ivy runs after him, but before I can follow, a car and three trucks whizz past.

"Jaxon!" I yell across the busy street. "*PLEASE?!*"

The desperation in my voice makes Ivy stop and reach for the box in Jaxon's hands, but he twists away, and with a wicked gleam in his eye, he shouts, "Sam, go long!" Then, as he does a perfect imitation of a referee's whistle, he lobs the box of hair dye like a football across First Street.

Running alongside parked cars, I open my arms to receive the missile coming my way. But it's Dad, not me, who's the football player in our family. The box bounces off my chest, drops into the street and splits open, sending the plastic bottle of coloring rolling out. Before I can get to it, the bottle rolls under the tire of a passing bus, and *splat!* Chestnut-brown hair dye squirts all over the pavement and even some of the parked cars. By the time the bus passes, Jaxon and Ivy are gone.

As I stare in horror at the flattened box and the explosion of dye that's seeping into the roadway, my head aches with a horrid realization. In my backpack, there's only enough money—*exactly* enough money—for the rest of the things I have to purchase. Yet I don't dare return to Mr. Wells's with only fourteen items.

I consider throwing myself in front of the next bus.

I consider marching right back into Colodner's Drugstore and shoplifting a second box of hair dye. But I promised Mr. Wells that I wouldn't do anything illegal, so I have to keep considering.

Finally, I make a new plan. Squaring my shoulders, I step back onto the sidewalk, point myself toward stop #2—Hopkins Hardware—and set off on the rest of the Red Mission.

Like a hot knife through soft butter, I move through the next fourteen assignments on my memorized list. As I go from store to store in downtown Nickel Bay, I pass the paper-covered windows of so many other businesses and restaurants that didn't survive. In each store I visit, I follow Mr. Wells's advice. I scope out the surveillance cameras. I avoid eye contact with the staff. And I take my purchases to cash registers that are staffed by temporary employees who've never seen me before. The only person who recognizes me is old Mr. Tuck, who owns Wonderland, the toy and game store.

"Hey, there's my buddy!" he shouts the minute I walk in the door.

"Hey, Mr. Tuck," I call out.

"Did ya have a good Christmas, Bob?" he asks. "And how about those pretty sisters of yours?"

Mr. Tuck is at least five years older than dust, so he's

not real great in the memory department. A few years back he decided that my name is either Bob or Arnie and that I've got two or three sisters. So I don't worry about him remembering that I'm here today to buy a pack of playing cards.

Once I make my final purchase—a shrink-wrapped tin of Altoids breath mints from the Nickel Bay Newsstand and Confectionery—I have spent every last penny Mr. Wells handed me the day before. But now I need an additional $3.95 to replace the purchase that got squished under the wheels of the First Avenue bus. I check the time. Ten thirty. I have a half hour to buy another hair dye and still get to Mr. Wells's back door by eleven.

Through potholed alleys and backyards, I race home. Once there, I slip off my now-bulging backpack and tear through our apartment, digging for coins in the backs of kitchen drawers (one nickel), under the cushions of the living room couch (one dime), and behind Dad's easy chair (three pennies). I turn my long-neglected piggy bank on its head and shake out the coin I can hear banging around in there. A lonely quarter.

Which brings my grand total to forty-three cents.

"Think, Sam! Think!" I mutter to myself until I whirl and see, in an alcove above the refrigerator, the answer to my problem.

Our penny jar.

The penny jar was Mom's idea. "Every penny is another wish that will come true," she used to say right up until she left.

"Yeah, well, you can see how well that worked out," Dad grumbled after Mom was gone. Then he stuck the penny jar on top of the fridge, where nobody ever fed it another cent.

Climbing the kitchen stepladder, I reach the dusty, heavy jar and carefully lower it to the counter, where I count out three hundred and fifty-two pennies. Added to the forty-three cents I found earlier, I now have exactly $3.95. I sweep the coins into a sandwich baggie, screw the lid back on the penny jar and replace it above the fridge.

All those coins—and the fourteen purchases from earlier—jostle in my knapsack and bang on my spine as I race downtown. It's only when I turn the corner at Griffin and Eighth that a horrible thought hits me, and I stop in the middle of the sidewalk.

I'm not supposed to be noticed. Yet only a blind salesclerk with the IQ of a meatball would fail to notice a scrawny, sweaty kid who's trying to pay for a box of chestnut-brown women's hair dye with almost four hundred pennies.

How could I be so stupid?

I brace my hands on my knees and sag, panting white clouds of vapor into the gray late-morning air. My eyes dart this way and that. And then I spot salvation. Directly across the street, with a sign in its window that screams MUST CLOSE!! LAST FOUR DAYS!! is a branch of Nickel Bay Savings and Loan. Is there any better place than a bank to turn pennies into paper money?

Five minutes later, I stop around the corner from Colodner's Drugstore, ready to complete my shopping list. The thief in me knows that I've got to change my appearance just enough that nobody in the store will wonder why the same kid in the same jacket and knit cap is back buying the same hair dye he bought an hour and a half ago. So I whip off my cap, stuff it in my pocket, and turn my winter coat inside out. Clutching the three dollar bills, three quarters, and two dimes in my right hand, I stride into Colodner's, a man on a mission.

The Red Mission.

THE BENJAMINS IN THE BACKPACK

"Now we just have to let the ink dry." Mr. Wells sits back in his wheelchair, wearing white cotton gloves. In front of him, stretching down the middle of a long wooden worktable, is a row of fifteen hundred-dollar bills, all of them stamped with a purple phoenix. The sight of all those Nickel Bay Bucks stops me in my tracks, but Mr. Wells snaps me back to reality with, "How'd it go, Sam?"

"Huh?" After my frantic last-minute rescue of the Red Mission, I'm still a little shaken up. "Fine. Yeah, fine," I mutter, hoisting my knapsack onto the table.

We're in a huge workroom lit by bright fluorescent lights in Mr. Wells's basement. All sorts of tools hang from the walls. Some I recognize, like table saws, electric drills and sanding machines. But there are other contraptions I've never seen before.

From across the table Mr. Wells, Dr. Sakata and Hoko watch intently as I unzip my backpack, pull each item from its shopping bag and place it behind a corresponding Benjamin. I keep waiting for some sort of response, some sign of approval, but Mr. Wells is silent. When I'm done, my purchases are lined up and down the table like little soldiers.

Mr. Wells rolls along, scanning the display, while overhead, the fluorescent bulbs hum. When he gets to the hair dye, he leans forward and tips the box back as if to study the label. "Did you have any . . . problems?" Why he's asking me that while examining the hair dye is kind of creepy, but I shake off the feeling that he's reading my mind.

"Problems? Nope. No problems."

Mr. Wells wheels back to the head of the table, where he gently touches the purple ink on one of the bills, examines his finger and smiles. He holds it up to Dr. Sakata, who also smiles and nods. I'm feeling left out. "What're you guys looking at?"

Mr. Wells points the clean white fingertip at me.

"Ink's dry!" he exclaims.

After Dr. Sakata slips on his own pair of white gloves, he and Mr. Wells prep the worktable like doctors getting ready for surgery. They lay out an assortment of tools, some with different-size blades, others with curved or corkscrew tips. They line up stacks of tissues, boxes of cotton balls, and piles of sandpaper. Finally they strap magnifying glasses embedded with intense little lightbulbs around their foreheads.

And then they begin.

A few of the boxes I've bought are easy to get into. With the toothpaste carton, for instance, Mr. Wells simply opens the flap, slides a folded Nickel Bay Buck inside and closes it. But most of the items are specially wrapped, and that's where all the equipment comes in.

The box of playing cards, for instance, is sealed at both ends by glued-on paper stamps and encased in cellophane. With a pointed razor blade, Mr. Wells carefully cuts away the cellophane while Dr. Sakata fills an electric teapot with water. When steam starts rising from the kettle's spout, Mr. Wells repeatedly waves the box of cards through the column of steam as he slowly—very slowly—loosens one paper stamp with a blunt little spatula. Once he's able to open that end of the box and slip a folded bill inside, he moistens the stamp in the cloud of steam and reseals the box flap.

Then comes the cool part.

Dr. Sakata plugs in a machine that looks like a miniature waffle iron. While waiting for that to heat up, he carefully measures and cuts a rectangle from a roll of clear cellophane and hands it to Mr. Wells, who centers the box of cards on the transparent film. In a blur of hand movements that I can't even follow, he folds, twists and pleats the cellophane around the box until it fits like a second skin. Then he quickly presses it between the heated plates of Dr. Sakata's toaster, sealing the cellophane . . . spins the box so it's standing on end . . . presses it one last time . . . and I can't believe my eyes! The box of cards looks the way it did when it left the factory.

Mr. Wells catches me watching him with my jaw hanging open.

"Yes, Sam?"

I shake my head in admiration. "You must have been a really great spy," is all I can think to say.

"I've told you, I wasn't a spy," he reminds me.

"Well, whatever you were, you must've been real good at it."

He makes a tiny nod and continues with his work. The first five or six insertions are pretty interesting, but then I start getting restless.

"Do I have to stay for all of this?" I ask.

"Are you expected somewhere else?"

I shrug. "No. But I'm bored now."

That makes him look up. "You're *bored?*" He pulls off his magnifying spectacles and glares at me. "You are the featured player in one of the most intricate and longest-running mysteries in the history of espionage, and you're *bored?!*"

"I'm not really doing anything," I mumble. "I don't have white gloves, and I don't really know how to use your tools. Or even what they're for."

"Then you can tell me a story."

"A story?" I screw up my face. "What makes you think I can tell a story?"

"Because you're a good liar, Sam." Before I can object,

he says, "You demonstrated that the night you fell from my roof and lied to your father on the phone."

I shift uncomfortably on my feet.

"So . . . tell me a story."

"What kind of story?"

"I don't care." He shrugs. "Tell me about your heart operation."

"I was unconscious."

"Okay. Tell me a memory you have of your mother."

"She left me and Dad right before I turned four, and now she's remarried. End of story." I fold my arms across my chest and squeeze my lips together. If he thinks he's getting any more out of me, he's mistaken.

"Okay. Maybe not one of your own stories, then," Mr. Wells says. "Tell me something about this town I don't know."

I squint in thought before I answer. "You know how Nickel Bay got its name?" He shakes his head. "Okay. I'll tell you that story," I say, "but on one condition."

"Which is?"

"You tell me one."

He studies me before he nods. "It's a deal."

So I begin.

"More than a hundred years ago, this area around the bay was called some Indian name that was so long that nobody could pronounce it. All there was at the water's edge were a couple of wooden shacks owned by a fur

103

trapper named Sly Guffson, who also happened to be a sneaky card-playing gambler. Any stranger passing through these parts, Mr. Guffson would challenge them to what he called"—with my fingers, I make air quotes—"'a friendly game of cards.' And he'd always win. Until the night he invited three travelers to 'a friendly game of cards' without knowing that one of them was a frontier preacher who also happened to be a card shark. His name was Phineas Wackburton."

Mr. Wells looks startled. "That was his real name?"

"That's what the history books say."

Mr. Wells laughs and mutters, "Phineas Wackburton," as he goes back to work.

"Mr. Wackburton started by letting the other three players win a few deals, but then he stepped up his game and started raking in the cash. When Sly Guffson realized that Mr. Wackburton knew as many dirty poker tricks as he did, he got madder and madder. After playing all night, Mr. Wackburton had stacks of coins in front of him, and the other three players were down to only a nickel apiece. Still, they all insisted on playing one final hand, and to do that, each guy had to toss a nickel into the pot. Four nickels, twenty cents total. Once the cards were dealt, the other two men folded, and that left the fur trader, Mr. Guffson, facing off against the preacher, Phineas Wackburton.

"Seeing his opponent had no money left, Phineas

pushed all his winnings into the center of the table, figuring that his bet would force Mr. Guffson to fold. But Guffson thought his hand was unbeatable. Plus, he was hopping mad and kinda drunk, so he did something pretty boneheaded. He wagered his land, his two wooden shacks and a little dock he had built out into the bay."

"He bet everything he owned on a hand of poker?" Mr. Wells asks.

"Everything. Except the mule that he rode out of town on after he lost."

Mr. Wells chuckles and continues his work.

"Then, as the town started to grow, Phineas Wackburton framed the four nickels he won in that poker game and hung them in the first saloon he opened here. That's when people started calling the place Nickel Bay. And those nickels became famous."

"Are they still around?" Mr. Wells wonders.

"A few." I count on my fingers as I talk. "One was given to President William McKinley when he came through Nickel Bay back in 1900. But a couple days later he mistakenly mixed it in with his pocket change and used it to buy a hot dog in Philadelphia."

"A hot dog!" Mr. Wells barks. "Imagine."

"The second nickel was sent away to some ginormous museum in Washington, DC . . ."

"The Smithsonian?"

"Yeah, probably," I quickly agree. "The third coin is on

exhibit in a bulletproof case at the Nickel Bay Historical Society. And the fourth one . . . the fourth nickel is . . . I mean *was* . . ."

My voice cracks, and I suddenly stop talking. Mr. Wells, Hoko and Dr. Sakata all look to me.

"What is it?" Mr. Wells asks.

Everyone else in town knows where the fourth nickel went, so I've never had to tell this story before. I don't know why I'm choking up, but I cough like I've got something in my throat and continue.

"You remember I told you how Dad saved all those people in the fire, and everybody was calling him a hero?"

Mr. Wells nods.

"Well, to honor him, the town council threw a huge ceremony. Seriously, thousands of people were there, and the mayor gave my dad the fourth nickel. All framed and everything."

"You must have been very proud."

I shrug. "I was too little to remember."

"So this fourth nickel," Mr. Wells says, "where does your father keep it? In a safety deposit box, I bet."

"He lost it."

"*Lost* it?"

"Let's just say: It got lost. After Dad was laid off by the fire department, and after the divorce and after my operation, Dad and me, we kept moving as the money ran out. And somewhere along the way . . . *poof!*" I explode my hands. "Gone."

"Well, I'm sorry to hear that," Mr. Wells says before slipping a Nickel Bay Buck between the pages of a popular novel I bought at Brandt Brothers Bookstore. He slides the book to the middle of the table, and I can see that he and Dr. Sakata have finished hiding all fifteen one-hundred-dollar bills inside my purchases.

He removes his magnifying-glass headgear and says something foreign to Dr. Sakata, who leaves the room. Mr. Wells pushes his wheelchair back from the table and stretches his arms above his head.

"Time for lunch, don't you think?" he asks.

"What about your story?"

"My story will have to wait, Sam," Mr. Wells says. "After lunch, you've got a full afternoon of pickpocket training."

The good news is that Hoko no longer seems focused on eating me. During lunch, he sits attentively at my elbow, watching every spoonful of soup travel to my mouth, but he doesn't growl once.

The bad news is that I still suck at pickpocketing.

"We should have begun this training at Thanksgiving," Mr. Wells finally grumbles in the late afternoon, shaking his head. Then he turns to Dr. Sakata, and I know he's repeating himself because the sentence he speaks ends with "Thanksgiving."

Dr. Sakata glances my way and nods gravely.

I shout, "I'm in the room, you know!" and the frustration that's been building bubbles over. "Maybe I'm not an expert pickpocket yet, but don't forget—this morning I got you *every* item you asked for! But do you appreciate it? Apparently not. Do I get one word of encouragement? Not one that I heard!"

Mr. Wells lets my anger subside before he speaks softly.

"Forgive me, Sam, if I don't throw a parade every time you do the work you've been assigned. This morning, you did your job. No more, no less. When you go above and beyond what's asked of you—if, for instance, you ever demonstrate that you've mastered the skill of pickpocketing—then Dr. Sakata and I will be the first to applaud."

I chew on my bottom lip, still steaming, but Mr. Wells changes the subject abruptly.

"All right, then! Tomorrow's the fourth day of Christmas. And that's *especially* important because it's what?" He looks to me.

I answer automatically, "The return of Nickel Bay Nick."

"Precisely. Now, my housekeeper comes tomorrow, and I don't want to take the chance of her seeing you here. So . . ." He rolls back to the worktable and indicates the store-bought items in front of us. "You'll take these with you this evening and leave from your home in the morning. Do you understand?"

I gulp. "You're trusting me with all this money overnight?"

He looks me in the eye. "I will trust you until you give me a reason not to. Do I make myself clear?"

And though my stomach tightens at the thought of all those Nickel Bay Bucks in my care, I meet his gaze and answer, "Crystal."

"Good." Mr. Wells pulls on his cotton gloves, I slip on my own winter gloves, and together we carefully load my backpack with more money than I have ever dreamed of having in my possession.

THE RETURN OF A LEGEND
December 28–29

The second I walk in the front door, my cell phone goes off. It's Jaxon. "What do you want?" I bark as I remove my Rolex and hide it—along with my full knapsack—in the back of my bedroom closet.

"Yo, yo, Samwich!" Jaxon starts in, like he doesn't have a care in the world. "Ivy and me, we're gonna crash the new three-D movie at the Angel Street Cinema tonight. Wanna come be our lookout?"

"Be your own lookouts," I snarl.

That makes Jaxon laugh. "Whoa! You're not upset about that thing with the hair dye, are you?"

"I had to buy a second box and pay for it myself!"

"So, sue me!" Jaxon squeals. "My dad's a lawyer, and he'll kick your butt all over the courtroom."

People in Nickel Bay whisper that Jaxon's dad got famous and rich by keeping a lot of bad guys out of jail.

Jaxon loves to drop that fact about a jillion times in every conversation.

Just then, I hear Dad come through the front door. I close my closet and say, "I gotta go," as I snap the phone shut.

"Hey, Sam," Dad calls. "How was your day?"

"Oh, y'know," I yell back.

He leans into my bedroom. "No, I *don't* know. That's why I'm asking."

"Well, let me tell you, then," I say, folding my arms. "Today I moved and alphabetized all the files starting with *F* and *G*. The *F* boxes were a real snooze, but, man! Those *G* files were mind-blowing!" I smile sweetly. "And how was your day?"

"No need to be snide," Dad grumbles as he walks away.

That night we eat mac 'n' cheese without saying a word. After I take my seven-thirty pill, I hang out in my bedroom, pretending to read, but my gaze keeps drifting to my closet door. I'm so distracted that when Dad pops in just before bedtime and says, "Don't forget . . ." I jump about three feet out of my chair.

"Jeez!" I yelp.

"Sorry," Dad says. "Didn't mean to scare you."

"You didn't," I sniff. "What did you say?"

"Don't forget," he says, "we've got Mrs. Atkinson tomorrow."

"I didn't forget."

The truth is, I had totally forgotten. The same way I forgot our last appointment in early December. And then, when Dad called me and I showed up late, he started in on me. I got so upset that I ran out of the room and climbed through the little trapdoor in the elevator ceiling. Then I spent the next two hours on the roof of the elevator, riding up and down in the shaft, while security guards scoured the building looking for me. My snickering finally gave away my location. Mrs. Atkinson is still furious.

"But tomorrow's Saturday," I point out. "How come she's working on a weekend?"

"Everybody at Town Hall's working Saturday," Dad explains. "It's to make up for the Christmas holiday."

"What a drag," I grunt, and turn back to my desk.

"Do I need to call Mr. Wells?" Dad asks.

"Call him?" I whirl around. "For what?"

"So you can get off work. For our appointment."

"Oh." For a second there, I was certain my cover was blown. I was sure Dad had somehow figured out I'm hiding a small fortune about four feet from where he's standing.

"Mr. Wells? Nah. I'll tell him."

Mom used to sing me to sleep when I was little, so I pretend to hear her voice in my head as I toss and turn that night. But even that doesn't work. Between the money in the closet and the job I've got to do in the morning, I can't stop twitching. Once the digital clock next to my bed clicks to 12:01 a.m., however, I whisper, "The fourth day of Christmas," and finally doze off.

In the morning I shuffle around the apartment, burping a lot and bumping into walls, pretending I'm still half asleep. I'm eating my cereal over the kitchen sink when Dad blows past on his way out.

"Don't you have a job to get to?" he calls over his shoulder, but he doesn't wait for an answer.

Dumping the cereal bowl in the sink, I shift into high gear. From a mountain of dull-colored clothes on my bed, I pick out the day's disguise, and as I get dressed, I notice my fingers are shaking. *I'm never this nervous when I'm actually going to steal things,* I find myself thinking.

Two minutes to nine. From across the street, I stare at the front door of Colodner's Drugstore with steely determination. I check the laces on my shoe, adjust the knapsack over my shoulder and slow my breathing. Finally I extend one hand, palm down, in front of my eyes, and very softly, I sing the song Mom taught me in Memphis.

My heart is strong
My hands are steady
My future waits
And now I'm ready
Whoa-oh
I'm so ready

I look at my wristwatch, and you know what time it is? Time for the return of Nickel Bay Nick.

Colodner's Drugstore is nearly empty, but as I turn into the hair care aisle, I'm startled to find a clerk down on one knee, restocking the shelves in the exact spot where I need to place my purchase. I stroll past, desperate to create a distraction, and at the other end of the aisle, I spy an opportunity. An old lady not much taller than me is inching her cart along, squinting back and forth between the shopping list in her left hand and the store shelves. As she passes, with one foot I nudge the front of her cart toward a display of salted peanuts, and she doesn't notice that she's on a collision course until it's too late. The moment the tower of cans crashes to the floor, the clerk jumps up to clear the mess, giving me the opening I need to swoop in and make my drop.

After visiting a few more stores, I make a valuable realization: overweight people in overstuffed winter coats provide the best cover. Walking alongside one of them, I'm hidden from store clerks and surveillance cameras, and it's a snap for me to reach into my half-unzipped backpack, grab an appropriate item, and then—*plunk!*—replace it on its original shelf.

By the time I exit Wise Automotive Supplies, the fifth store on my route, I'm feeling pretty pleased with myself. But that glow quickly disappears when I see the Bunster brothers heading in my direction.

I've shared the backseat of many police cars with Lyle and Spaldo Bunster. The Bunsters snatch purses. And briefcases. And fanny packs. Then they run. Which is why they wear tennis shoes, even in the winter.

Normally, the Bunsters wouldn't be in my neighborhood, but in this economy, I'm guessing they've picked the streets clean on the other side of the bay, over where people live in nicer houses and drive bigger cars.

The few who can still afford to.

And normally the Bunsters wouldn't give me a second glance, but I can tell from the way their eyes widen when they see me that they're also seeing my bulging backpack. Lyle—the skinnier one—nudges Spaldo and thrusts his chin in my direction. Spaldo nods, as if to say *I see it,* and they slow down.

I slow down, too.

The brothers look around. Nobody's coming. They take a few quick breaths, high-five each other and start running *straight at me*!

Now, my brain realizes that I've still got a thousand dollars in my bag and that I should probably be scramming very quickly in the opposite direction, but my feet don't get that message. Instead, I freeze like a squirrel in front of a speeding car on a country road, and my pulse shoots up to about a thousand. The Bunster brothers are approaching fast, and in the next second I expect to feel the knapsack ripped from my shoulder as they whiz past. But just as Lyle and Spaldo get close enough that

I can see the tattoos on their necks, a Christmas miracle happens.

From an alley between the Bunsters and me, out steps . . . Dr. Sakata.

When he turns to face the brothers and folds his arms across his massive chest, he looks like a brick wall in a black suit. I hear the squeal of tennis shoes on shoveled pavement as Lyle and Spaldo screech to a halt. Their jaws drop, and in the next split second, they spin on their rubber heels and disappear around a distant street corner.

Without even a glance in my direction, Dr. Sakata crosses the street. I blink in disbelief and relief at what just happened—or, rather, *didn't* just happen—and by the time I open my eyes, Dr. Sakata is gone.

I shake off my daze and race to my next drop-off, but on the way, the questions begin. How did Dr. Sakata happen to be in the right place at the right time? Or was he following me? Doesn't Mr. Wells trust me? Or was he just making sure that nothing happens to his fifteen hundred dollars?

I'd never give Mr. Wells the satisfaction of hearing this from me, but all his training sure pays off. I remember the exact order of every store to visit. I remember the exact shelf where each item in my knapsack belongs. I remember to turn up my collar and to keep my head down.

An hour later, after I smoothly return the deck of playing cards to its place on the sales table at Wonderland Toy Shop, only one item remains in my bag, and I'm feeling pretty psyched. Out on the street, I'm allowing my-self a little fist pump and a quiet "Yessss!" when my cell phone suddenly plays Dad's ring tone. I check my watch. It's only eleven fifteen.

"It's too early for my pill," I grumble into the phone.

"Where are you?" Dad sounds mad.

Uh-oh. He expects me to be in Mr. Wells's basement or attic. Thinking fast, I duck into a recessed doorway so Dad won't hear any traffic noises.

"I'm at work." I try to sound cool. "Where I'm supposed to be."

"You're *supposed* to be at Town Hall for our eleven o' clock session with Mrs. Atkinson."

I almost swallow my tongue. "Oh, no."

"Oh, yes!" Dad snaps. "Now, are you coming, or do I have to drive over to Mr. Wells's and drag you out myself?"

"I'm on my way!" I slam the phone shut and agonize. I've still got to return the tin of Altoids to Nickel Bay Newsstand and Confectionery, but that'll take me four blocks out of the way. I'm only two blocks from Town Hall right now.

This is what you call a no-brainer.

As I run, I remember to remove my Rolex and hurriedly zip it into the front pocket of my knapsack. When I dash into Town Hall, Dad's waiting right inside the revolving door. "I'm sorry, I'm sorry, I'm sorry," I huff and puff, and my voice echoes in the two-story marble lobby. Instead of responding, Dad swings his eyes upward, giving me a signal. I follow his gaze and find Mrs. Atkinson standing at the mezzanine railing, looking down at me and shaking her head. She pulls a pencil from her hair bun, checks her wristwatch and scribbles in her notebook.

Clapping me on the shoulder, Dad groans, "Let's get this over with," before he turns and crosses the floor. I start to follow, but when I see what stands between me and the main staircase, I freeze.

Five feet ahead, two uniformed guards beckon visitors through a metal detector, while two more study the X-ray screens at the end of a conveyor belt.

How could you forget the security checkpoint? I scream inside my skull. If I put my bag on the conveyor belt, I realize, the X-ray will definitely see my Rolex . . . and the tin of mints! The guards might ignore the watch, but I'm scared that they're going to be curious about a rectangular metal object. And when they unzip my bag, Dad's going to be standing there, wondering what I'm doing with the Rolex that's supposed to be up in . . .

"You coming or what?" Dad's voice snaps me into focus. He has already cleared the metal detector and is waiting impatiently on the other side.

I don't even realize I've stopped in the middle of the lobby floor. Panicked, I look around. Above me Mrs. Atkinson taps her pencil in exasperation. Straight ahead, Dad clenches his jaw. From beyond the security barriers, the guards await my next move.

The dull boom of my own heartbeat fills my ears as I set my backpack down on the conveyor belt. "You have to let go," one of the security guards points out, and he's right. My fist is still gripping the shoulder strap. When I open my hand, the bag slides forward, and time slows to a crawl. I feel every eye in the room boring into my skull, reading my mind and learning my secret identity. As my bag passes through the rubber flaps and out of sight, I have a final, terrible thought. *What if Mr. Wells gets so upset that he decides to feed me to Hoko?*

At that very moment, the quiet of the lobby is shattered by a sudden scream. And guess what?

I'm not the one who's screaming.

From out of a mezzanine hallway, a plump older woman comes running, shrieking like the hounds of hell are after her. In one hand she waves a mini TV as she wails, "Oh my word! Have you seen the news?" She nearly collides with Mrs. Atkinson before she stops at the head of the staircase, thrusts her TV overhead and shouts to the crowd below, "He's back! *Nickel Bay Nick is back!*"

A cheer erupts from every throat in the room. Some people jump up and down, while others high-five each other. Complete strangers embrace, and one woman crosses herself and mutters a prayer. It's always like this, every time Nickel Bay Nick first shows up, but this year—maybe because it's later than usual—people seem extra happy.

While everyone's distracted, I glance over to the

security area, where I can see the skeleton of my back-pack—with its cargo of the tin box and my wristwatch—gliding across the unwatched X-ray screen. I step through the unattended metal detector to reclaim my bag, and when I turn around to join Dad, he grabs me, spins me around . . . and hugs me. He smells like cupcake frosting.

And for the first time in a really long time, I hug him back.

THE SOUND OF CELEBRATION

Chattering employees clog the hallways of Town Hall, passing around stale Christmas cookies and uncorking bottles of unchilled champagne. From what I can overhear, the first report of Nick's return came from Brandt Brothers Bookstore, where a lady found what she thought was a bookmark in the bestseller she was browsing through.

Then she saw the purple phoenix.

When she started yelling, the store manager called the police, and once they arrived and saw the Nickel Bay Ben, they alerted the media.

Pushing through the crowd, Mrs. Atkinson tries unsuccessfully to lead me and Dad back to her office. Finally, clearly annoyed, she turns and shouts over the noise, "In light of today's events, maybe we should reschedule our appointment."

121

Out on the street, Dad starts his car and rolls down the window. "People seem pretty excited, huh?" he says, nodding toward Town Hall. "Nickel Bay Nick reappearing like that."

"I guess," I grunt, trying to appear bored. I squint into the distance as Dad's car idles.

"Can I run you back over to Mr. Wells's?"

"Nah," I say, scuffing at a mound of dirty snow, "I could use the exercise."

"Well, okay," Dad says. "See you at home later."

I wait until he turns a corner before I head off to replace the box of breath mints at Nickel Bay Newsstand and Confectionery. The five or six people in the store are gathered around a television at the front counter, too busy talking about Nick's return to pay any attention to me.

Out on the sidewalk, I sag against a fire hydrant and contemplate my next move. My backpack is empty. My work is done. I've got nobody to celebrate with, and even if I did, I couldn't tell them what it is we're celebrating. Finally, with a sigh, I trudge on.

But in front of Buzzetti's Electronics, I stop and stare.

The seven TVs in the window display are tuned to seven different channels, and each channel is carrying a different news story about shoppers finding Nickel Bay Bucks at one of the stores I'd visited that morning. Across the bottoms of the screens are banners saying things like

NICK! WHAT TOOK YOU SO LONG? or **NICK HASN'T FORGOTTEN NICKEL BAY!** while onscreen, people excitedly wave hundred-dollar bills at the camera, laughing or crying with joy. Then, like a piano dropped from a ten-story building, the realization hits me:

I did that.

With everything going on at Town Hall—seeing Dad mad, panicking about the X-ray machine, hearing the cheers of the workers—it hadn't sunk in yet. But I now realize . . .

I'm Nickel Bay Nick.

I know Nick is Mr. Wells's invention. And it's his money and his plan. But this year, right now, *I'm* Nick.

I exhale and stagger backward a little. My head swims, and I smile the biggest, stupidest smile I've smiled in a long time.

Fifteen minutes later, I'm pounding with both fists on Mr. Wells's back door and getting ready to stab the bell for the third time when the door flies open. Before I can yell, *"Do you believe it?"* Dr. Sakata grabs me by the collar, quickly looks around outside and drags me in. Mr. Wells is waiting right inside the door.

"What are you doing here?" he demands.

"Have you seen the news?" I start blabbering. "People are buying our stuff and finding the money, and holy cow! I was just downtown, and it's getting crazy! There's all this traffic in the streets, and people all over the sidewalks and—"

"Sam!" Mr. Wells slams his fist on his wheelchair's armrest. "Why are you here?"

I stop and blink. "Because it's working. Just like we planned!"

"That's why it's called *a plan*!" Mr. Wells tries to calm his voice. "And part of that plan was that you were not to be seen here on the day of Nickel Bay Nick's reappearance."

I suddenly remember. "Oh, right! Your housekeeper." I lower my voice. "She still here?"

"Fortunately, she'd just gone out the front when you began your racket at the back door."

"Sorry," I mutter.

"Never, *ever* drop by unannounced!" He rolls closer. "Three times a day, I let Hoko out to have the run of the backyard. What would happen, do you think, if you surprised him? Do you think he would hesitate to chase you down like a rabbit?"

As if to emphasize Mr. Wells's threat, Hoko casually yawns and licks his massive chops.

"I said I was sorry."

Mr. Wells shakes his head and starts to wheel away.

"Did you have Dr. Sakata follow me?" I call after him.

Mr. Wells slowly turns. "What do you think? Do you think Dr. Sakata was out shopping the after-Christmas sales for bedroom slippers? And that he just happened to pass by as you found yourself in danger?" Before I can answer, he plunges ahead. "Or didn't you think that I would take every possible step to insure that you and your backpack and *our entire operation* were not endangered by any unforeseen circumstances? *That's* why it's called a plan."

"Okay, okay," I mutter. "I thought maybe it's because you don't trust me."

"What have I said before, Sam? I will trust you until you give me a reason not to." He tilts his head and looks at me. "Should I be concerned?"

"No," I mumble, staring at the floor.

Since I'm already there, Mr. Wells decides I should stay for lunch, and as we sip our broccoli soup in the kitchen, I decide that this might be a good time to start uncovering a few of Mr. Wells's secrets.

"Where'd you get all the money?" I ask casually.

I guess that catches him by surprise, because Mr. Wells spits a little jet of soup back into his bowl, runs his napkin across his mouth and clears his throat. "I beg your pardon?"

"All the money you give away. Did you smuggle, like, gold and stuff out of India and all those places where you lived?"

"My personal finances are hardly your concern."

"But that's not fair."

"What's not fair?"

"You know practically everything there is to know about me. I even told you about my Hanuman," I say, touching the figure at my neck. "But I know diddly about you."

"Information is power," he says with a shrug. "My game. My rules." Then he goes back to eating.

I shake my head. "Were you like this with your kids?"

He looks up. "Come again?"

"You told me and Dad you had kids. A girl and a boy, right?"

"That's correct."

"So, is this how you talked to them when they had questions?"

Mr. Wells's face suddenly goes slack, and the spoon in his hand starts to tremble. After a long pause, he sets it down and speaks quietly.

"You asked about my money. In my very long career, I served in a total of fourteen countries all over Southeast Asia. I worked with and earned the confidence of emperors and presidents and even kings. At various times, I was called upon to save lives, to free hostages and to resolve potentially explosive situations. And, yes, there were occasions—after a crisis was averted, let's say, or a loved one returned home safely—when I would be surprised with a gift, some sort of thank-you, from a foreign head of state or a grateful billionaire. But I honestly never paid much attention to these demonstrations of gratitude. I put those jewels and gold coins and engraved platinum watches into safekeeping and moved on to the next job. And the next one. And the next.

"That was all my life was about back then. My job. My children would be the first to tell you that I was often . . . absent." He stops for a moment, as though lost in a memory. Then he continues. "It wasn't until my wife passed away and I found myself wondering what to do with the rest of my life that I took inventory of the gifts I'd received over the years."

"By then you must've had a pile, huh?"

"A *pile*?" He smiles. "You could say that. And without a family to provide for any longer, I made the decision to share my"—he nods in my direction—"*pile* with the good people of Nickel Bay. Did that answer your question?"

I shrug. "Do you see your kids much?"

Mr. Wells freezes, staring across the table at me. Then he picks up his spoon and quietly announces, "Our soup is getting cold."

As we finish eating in silence, I begin to suspect that Mr. Wells is keeping more secrets than just Nickel Bay Nick. What other mysteries, I wonder, has he got locked away behind the walls of this big old house? I decide I'm going to stay alert and pick up whatever clues I can while I'm working for him. After all, what did he just say to me? "Information is power"?

I'd like to feel some of that power.

Once the lunch dishes are cleared, Mr. Wells makes me practice put-pocketing with Dr. Sakata, and as usual, I'm terrible. When we finally knock off at five thirty, I'm pretty discouraged, and as I'm pulling on my coat and grumbling under my breath, Mr. Wells asks, "What are you moping about, Sam?"

I sigh. "When I got here earlier, y'know? I was feeling awesome. I mean, Nickel Bay Nick is back, and I'm part of the reason people are jumpin' for joy. But after screwing up so badly at put-pocketing, now"—I lift my arms and let them drop to my side—"now I'm feeling I can't do anything right."

"That's why we keep training." He wheels closer to me. "But you should know, Sam, that your performance on the Red Mission was"—he searches for the right word and comes up with—"commendable."

I squint. "I don't know what that means."

"*Commendable*? It's a good word to know," he says. "It means 'worthy of praise.'"

For the first time since I've been working with Mr. Wells, he's said something that gives me a warm glow in my chest.

"'Worthy of praise,' huh?" I nod my head. "Okay. I'll take it."

"So, tomorrow, on the fifth day of Christmas," he says with vigor, "we'll begin laying the groundwork for the Green Mission."

"What's that going to be?"

"When you arrive in the morning, you'll find out," Mr. Wells says. "Meanwhile, you have the evening off. Enjoy yourself. Maybe even celebrate a little."

Whenever Nickel Bay Nick makes his first annual appearance, people go shopping. I'm sure some of them are hoping they'll score their very own Nickel Bay Ben, but most of them are just in a good mood, happy to get out and mingle. Even Dad had a good day at the bakery.

"Not great," he says when he gets home, "but better. Definitely better." He's so cheery that he doesn't even mind when Jaxon and Ivy show up.

"We heard that stores are staying open late on account of this Nickel Bay Nick thing," Jaxon explains to my dad, "so we figured we'd go hang out, y'know? Soak up some of that holiday spirit."

When he's around adults, Jaxon talks like a salesman on TV demonstrating steak knives.

"Can't," I announce. "I'm grounded."

"Why?" Jaxon turns to Dad with a curious smile. "Mr. Brattle? What'd Sam do that was so bad he got grounded?"

Dad turns to me. "Did I actually ground you?"

He hadn't, not really. But after what Jaxon pulled yesterday with the hair dye, I'm not feeling particularly chummy toward him. Then Ivy speaks. "But Nickel Bay Nick has come back! Can't you get un-grounded for one night?" One smile from her, and I usually melt like a sno-cone on a July sidewalk. This time is no exception.

As we head downtown, Jaxon wraps an arm around my shoulder. "You are just about the most awesome fifth-grader in history," he says in that charming way that always sucks me in.

"I am not," I scoff, and cast a sideways glance at Ivy.

"I'm serious! And you know what I admire most about you, Sammy?"

I shake my head.

"You know how to take a joke. Like that thing yester-day . . ."

And then he proceeds to reenact the scene outside Colodner's—doing all the parts, racing from the sidewalk into the street, playing keep-away with an imaginary box of hair dye and finally hurling it like a Hail Mary pass into my open, flailing arms. He's so funny that Ivy's laughing hysterically, and I'm finding it hard to stay mad. When Jaxon shouts, "And then remember—*SPLOOJ*?!" and makes the exact exploding sound of the bus rolling over the plastic dye bottle, I finally crack up, too.

"So, how's work going?" Ivy wants to know once we all stop giggling.

"Boring," I say quickly, anxious to change the subject. "What about you guys? How's your Christmas vacation been?"

But Jaxon doesn't want to talk about anything but my boss.

"That guy, Mr. Wells, he's pretty freaky deaky, huh?"

"Not really," I answer. "He's just quiet, that's all."

"He's got the prettiest dog," Ivy says. "Sometimes I see them over at Bayside Park."

"That's Hoko," I say.

"*Ho-Ko?*" Jaxon makes a sour face. "What kind of dumb name is Hoko?"

"It's not dumb," I insist.

"*Ho-o-o—Ko-o-o.*" Jaxon stretches the name out into one long whine. "Bet you could get quite a bundle for that mutt."

I stop in my tracks. "What did you say?"

"I'm talkin' about big bucks. Cha-ching!" he says, rubbing three fingers together. "My dad has a bunch of super-rich clients, y'know? And these guys collect all sorts of exotic animals."

"Like what?" Ivy asks.

"Like hairless cats and poisonous snakes. This one guy bought a huge lizard the size of a coffee table."

Ivy's eyes light up. "That was probably a Komodo dragon. They're enormous."

"Hey, Hoko is not for sale!" I snap.

"I never said he was!" Jaxon snaps back, but his flash of anger is gone in a second. Next thing you know, he's laughing and punching me playfully in the arm. "You're a tough little guy, aren't you?"

I smile tightly, trying to play along, but he's starting to push my buttons.

Ivy asks, "Jaxon? Your dad's clients . . . where do they get the lizards and snakes from?"

He drops his fists and shrugs. "I dunno about the lizards and stuff, but one of 'em was telling my dad about how much he wanted this really rare breed of cat he'd seen on TV. So my dad happens to mention it to Crummer." He turns to me. "You know Crummer? The dogcatcher?"

"Everybody knows Crummer Sikes," I say.

"Then, like, two weeks later, Crummer picks up that exact cat wandering the streets of Nickel Bay. No name tags or nothin'. Crummer made a nice chunk of change on that one."

Something in Jaxon's story bothers me. "Crummer just *happened* to find that same cat wandering around?"

"That's what he says." Jaxon pounds me on the back and chuckles. "Maybe Crummer's just lucky."

"If he were actually lucky," Ivy points out, "his parents wouldn't have named him Crummer."

They roar with laughter, but I'm not in a laughing mood anymore. "Y'know what, guys? I think I'm gonna head home."

Ivy groans, "Aw, come on, Sam," and Jaxon throws up his hands in exasperation. "*Now* what's wrong?"

"I just remembered," I lie, and hang my head for dramatic effect. "I don't have any money for dinner."

"Oh, please!" Jaxon snorts. "Since when do we pay? Let's go to that bowling alley where we ordered at the counter that one time. And when the food comes, we'll grab it and run like we did before, remember?"

The memory makes my stomach turn.

"That bowling alley's out of business," Ivy says.

"Maybe it's because of customers who didn't pay," I say sarcastically.

"Oh, boo-hoo," Jaxon sniggers. "That was a really good scam. We'll find someplace else and try it again."

But the thought of stealing my next meal doesn't seem like such an appealing idea.

"You've only been gone thirty minutes." Dad's puttering around in the kitchen when I get back. "Something wrong?"

"I didn't feel like hanging out," I say. "How come you're not with Lisa?"

"She got called in to work," Dad says. "After the news about Nickel Bay Nick, Dillard's stayed open tonight, so they temporarily rehired her."

I deliver my finest acting performance by simply grunting, "Cool."

Dad's always most relaxed when he's cooking at home, so while he makes chicken stew, I sit on the counter and we talk.

When he was still a firefighter, Dad got a lot of experience inventing recipes and preparing meals for the crews at the firehouse. After he was laid off, he figured he'd try to be a chef full-time, but once he realized that Nickel Bay wasn't a good place to start a restaurant, he bought a bakery for a good price and built a reputation for delicious breads and awesome cupcakes. "Cupcakes make people happy," he's always saying.

As we're eating Dad's stew, he casually says, "Your mom called right after you left. Checking in."

I don't look up.

"I told her you know about Phil."

My neck muscles tighten. "What did she say?"

"She wanted to know how you handled it. And if you'll ever forgive her."

"I haven't decided yet," I mutter, nudging a chunk of potato around on my plate.

"No rush," he says.

My chest burns, and I push my food away.

"Something wrong with the stew?" Dad asks.

"Nah," I say softly. "I'm just not very hungry."

Dad doesn't try to persuade me to finish my dinner. Instead, he picks up our plates and crosses to the sink. "If you ever want to talk about your mom—" he starts to say.

But I cut him off. "Yeah, yeah. I can always come to you. Whatever."

As exhausting as the day has been, I still lie awake later, wrestling with so many thoughts. Questions about Mom and her new life are pushed aside by questions about Mr. Wells and whatever secrets he's keeping. Jaxon's joking and Ivy's smile replay again and again. The great taste of Dad's stew still lingers on my tongue, and the cheering of those Town Hall workers rings in my ears until I finally drift off.

THE CHALLENGES OF CARJACKING
December 30

On Sunday, the fifth day of Christmas, the cease-fire between Dad and me doesn't last through breakfast.

"Tomorrow night's New Year's Eve," he announces. "Lisa's having a few people over, and I told her we'd be happy to be there."

"What do you mean, *we*?" I ask. "*I* won't be happy to be there."

"Well, you can't stay home," he says forcefully. "We both know what happened the last time I left you here alone on a holiday night."

"You mean Christmas? Christmas was different." I practically throw my cereal bowl in the sink. "That's when I found Mom's wedding picture you hid from me. And besides, I won't know anybody at Lisa's, and what if I have to work for Mr. Wells, and—"

"Stop!" Dad shouts. "You're coming. End of discussion. Did you take your meds?"

Defiantly staring him in the eye, I stick out my tongue and shove the pill to the back of my throat. On his way out of the kitchen, Dad adds, "And pick out something nice to wear to welcome in the New Year."

"Don't bother taking your coat off," Mr. Wells says when I arrive at eight thirty. "We're leaving immediately."

Dr. Sakata pulls on his gloves and helps Mr. Wells into a winter coat as Hoko gapes at all the activity with his tongue hanging out.

"Where're we going?"

"If you've been watching the news this morning," Mr. Wells says, tying a scarf around his neck, "you'll know that people are guessing about where Nickel Bay Nick will next appear." He turns to me with a wink. "Or, rather, *not* appear, if we do our job correctly. And I'm pleased to see there's one section of town that everyone's overlooking."

"Where's that?"

"The waterfront," he announces. "On the shores of Nickel Bay."

Back when Nickel Bay used to attract tourists, they'd all want to visit the area called Bay Front. From Bay Front Drive, you can get great views of the islands out in the water and the mountains on the opposite shore. Once the economy went south, though, even the most popular section of town lost a lot of businesses and residents.

As we pass through the kitchen, Dr. Sakata speaks quietly to Hoko, who immediately goes to curl up in his crate. Mr. Wells gathers maps and notepads on his way to the garage, where Dr. Sakata lifts him from his wheelchair into the front passenger seat of a hulking black SUV. I climb into the backseat and fasten my seat belt.

As we drive through the heart of town, I notice that, even though it's a super-cold, overcast Sunday, there's a lot more activity in the streets than I had seen only twenty-four hours earlier.

"Do you believe all these people?" I ask. "Nickel Bay Nick did that."

"But Nick still has two more missions ahead of him," Mr. Wells points out. "Now, tomorrow is December thirty-first, and you know what that means."

"New Year's Eve," I answer.

"Exactly. We can work early in the day, but I'm sending you home by mid-afternoon so that you can celebrate with your father."

"*Celebrate*?" I moan. "He's dragging me to his girlfriend's house."

"Is that so terrible?"

"Lisa's got two little girls. They're five and six, and they hang on me like monkeys on a banana tree."

"You're a brave man," Mr. Wells says, and I laugh. "Then Tuesday, the day after tomorrow," he continues, "you'll stay home."

"Do I have to?"

"Sam," Mr. Wells says, "nobody works on New Year's Day." I understand his point. "So," he continues, "we'll next see each other in the afternoon of Wednesday, January second."

"Why not Wednesday morning?"

"I'm having you start later that day because the Green Mission can only be carried out after dark."

"And what *is* the Green Mission?"

By now, we're rolling through Bay Front, only a couple blocks from Dad's bakery. This neighborhood actually comes to life—what little life there is anymore—after dark, when the neon signs flicker on and people gather in the bars and restaurants along the water's edge. But now the streets are sleepy, and FOR RENT signs are in the windows of a lot of empty shops.

"Three nights from now," Mr. Wells explains, "you will start at one end of Bay Front and work your way to the other. As you sneak along your route, you will slip fifteen one-hundred-dollar bills into fifteen parked cars."

"But what about cars that are locked?" I try to lean forward, but my seat belt yanks me back. "Or cars with alarms?"

Mr. Wells swivels in his seat to face me. "Didn't I see something in the police records about you stealing a car?"

"I already told you! It was my dad's car, and all I did was take his keys. Jaxon did the driving."

"What a shame. I thought you had more experience." He shrugs. "If you're going to be breaking into cars, you're going to have to learn the basics of being a car thief."

As Dr. Sakata drives up and down the side streets and

narrow alleys of Bay Front, Mr. Wells gives me a crash course in how to spot unlocked cars and how to avoid tripping burglar alarms. We pick out a street corner at the north end of Bay Front Drive where I will begin the Green Mission. "On the evening of January second, you will walk to this spot," Mr. Wells explains.

"Can't Dr. Sakata drive me?" I ask.

"He will pick you up when you're done," Mr. Wells says, "but I don't want this car to be observed in the area twice on the night of the Green Mission. I'm sure you can understand that."

"I guess," I grumble.

About a mile south, Mr. Wells points out another location—under the arch of a long-deserted church—where Dr. Sakata will meet me at the end of my mission. After more driving, Mr. Wells finally directs Dr. Sakata to pull into a garbage-strewn, snow-filled alley and stop.

"I want you to take the next few hours, Sam, to walk every possible route and make note of hazards and hiding places on this," he says, handing me a pencil and a map of Bay Front. "Now, do you have your cell phone with you?"

"Yeah, why?" I pull the phone from my jacket. "Who am I calling?"

"Please program this information into it," he says, holding up a piece of paper with a phone number on it. I do as he says, and then he tears up the paper. "When you've finished your scouting expedition, call that number, and I'll send Dr. Sakata to meet you at your pickup point."

"But it's cold out there," I protest.

"Then I suggest you zip up and start walking to keep warm."

It's only after the SUV pulls away that I realize I've been here before. In this exact spot. How do I know? On the brick wall in front of me, in letters three feet high, a slash of graffiti declares S.B. ROCKS!!!!!

Right where I spray-painted it two years before.

I only used my initials after Ivy pointed out that my full signature would probably earn me a visit from the police. Above my scrawl is a viper that Jaxon drew, and to the right is the pig with wings that Ivy did. I'd almost forgotten about that summer afternoon when the three of us swiped cans of spray paint from Hopkins Hardware and ran all over town, leaving our marks on any available surface. On that day, we couldn't stop laughing because we thought our tags looked so super-cool.

Now they just look dumb.

Did Mr. Wells let me out of his car right here because he wanted me to see my old graffiti? I wonder. *Is he deliberately rubbing my nose in my past? And if he is, how does he know so much about my life?*

I shiver, but this shiver has nothing to do with how cold it is.

By the time Dr. Sakata picks me up two hours later at our rendezvous, my fingers are stiff and my eyebrows are growing little icicles.

Back in Mr. Wells's kitchen, Dr. Sakata feeds me a bowl of clear soup with mushrooms and tiny shrimp floating in it. Normally, I'd turn up my nose at any meal that includes mushrooms and tiny shrimp, but I'm so cold that, at that moment, I'd be willing to drink lava.

Afterward, in his office, Mr. Wells spreads out my map of Bay Front and studies the route I traced between the buildings and down the side streets. As he does, I consider asking him whether he's deliberately sending me to the scenes of my previous crimes, but I'm not sure I want to hear his answer. Instead, I lean across the desk.

"I tried to avoid restaurants with bright lights out front," I point out, and he nods silently. "And if you look there"—I jab my finger at a spot on the map—"I'm gonna cut through the parking lot at Pirro's Pasta Palace. You think that's a good idea?"

"I'll trust your judgment." He looks up. "After all, this mission is a first for Nickel Bay Nick."

"What do you mean?"

"I mean that I have never done what I'm asking you to do."

I blink in surprise. "You've never tried this?"

"Even seven years ago, when I first acted as Nickel Bay Nick, I was not a young man," Mr. Wells explains. "I never had the speed or agility to slip in and out of shadows or crouch in dark doorways, waiting to strike."

Now he's got me worried. "How do you even know it can be done?"

"I don't," Mr. Wells says with a shrug. "But I do know that the job requires"—he counts on his fingers—"someone small in stature, someone fast on his feet and someone with the cold-blooded cunning of a cat burglar. You're more than qualified."

We spend the next few hours reviewing and revising the route that I devised through Bay Front. After that, I spend an hour practicing my miserable pickpocketing skills with Dr. Sakata, and by the end of the afternoon, my shoulders are slumped again.

"Tired, Sam?" Mr. Wells asks.

"This whole business of being mysterious," I say, "it's actually kind of exhausting, isn't it?"

"Ah!" Mr. Wells exclaims. "Now you know the dirty little secret about espionage. For every moment of hair-raising excitement and breathtaking adventure, there are ten thousand hours of mind-numbing preparation."

"Give me an example."

"Excuse me?"

"You owe me a story," I remind him. "You promised."

"Perhaps tomorrow," Mr. Wells protests. "It's late."

I throw my arms wide, the way I've seen him do, and flop back into a high-backed leather chair. "I've got all the time in the world."

So Mr. Wells clears his throat.

"Years ago, while I was stationed at the U.S. Embassy in a war-torn dictatorship, which shall remain nameless, one of our operatives—"

"*Operative*? Isn't that a fancy way of saying 'spy'?"

"*Spy* is . . . another word for what he was, yes." Mr. Wells nods. "Anyway . . . the identity of this operative had been—how should I put this?—compromised—"

"You mean somebody ratted him out," I suggest. "His cover was blown."

Mr. Wells scowls.

"I've seen spy movies," I say with a shrug. "I know how these things work."

"Do you want to tell the story?" Mr. Wells sounds annoyed.

I pull an imaginary zipper across my lips, and he continues.

"As I was saying, when our spy's cover was blown, he was in fear for his life. After narrowly avoiding capture by the dictator's army, he managed to slip into the capital city and take refuge in our embassy. The ambassador at the time was a cheerful but rather daffy older gentleman who spent more time obsessing about his six Saint Bernard dogs than he did worrying about matters of state. After the spy arrived, enemy soldiers surrounded the embassy and maintained surveillance twenty-four hours a day, determined to capture him. They checked every vehicle that entered and left the grounds. Then they began to confiscate all our food deliveries, and within just a few days, we were down to our last supplies and feeling like prisoners.

"The spy was desperate to flee to safety, and the ambassador was equally impatient to get him off the property.

But how could we manage that? All the generals and diplomats on staff, all of us were stumped, until I came up with a suggestion that sounded so crazy—"

"That it just might work," I chime in. Mr. Wells glares at me, and I immediately regret my words. "Sorry. They say that a lot in movies, too."

Mr. Wells goes on. "While in the country, I had made the acquaintance of a particularly gifted local tailor, a cheerful little man with one gold tooth and an amazing way with fabric. Through one of our kitchen workers, I sent a message to the tailor, who arrived the next day, bringing with him a large crate of toilet paper."

"Toilet paper?" I ask. "How are you supposed to save a spy with toilet paper?"

"Oh, the toilet paper was merely a fake-out," Mr. Wells answers. "Hidden in a false compartment at the bottom of that crate was a small sewing machine and twelve yards of a very special fabric the tailor had managed to smuggle in.

"Two days later, a pickup truck was stopped as it was leaving the embassy grounds, and it was searched by the dictator's soldiers. In the bed of the truck was a large, wooden dog crate, and through the slats of the cage, the soldiers could see one of the ambassador's Saint Bernards.

"'Why,' they demanded to know, 'is this dog leaving the property?'

"'Because,' I explained to the soldiers, 'she is pregnant and about to give birth.'"

145

I sit up. "Wait! What do you mean, *you* explained? Were you driving the truck?"

"I was."

"Were you in disguise?"

"From head to foot."

"Cool!" I exhale, and sit back.

"The dog was experiencing complications, I told the soldiers, and we were on our way to the animal clinic. 'So be careful,' I warned them. 'She might be disagreeable.' Of course, they ignored me and leaned in for a closer look. But when the dog lunged at them, growling and snapping, they quickly jumped back and waved me through."

"Did you get to the hospital in time?"

Mr. Wells wags a finger. "I was never headed for the hospital."

"You weren't?"

"Oh, no. Instead, I drove to a checkpoint at the country's border, where we transferred the crate to another of our government's trucks waiting just on the other side of the border crossing."

"Why did you send that poor, pregnant dog out of the country?"

"Because as soon as that crate crossed the border, our agents on the other side opened it and released . . . our spy."

I couldn't believe my ears. "You put your spy in a crate *with an angry, pregnant Saint Bernard*?"

"Sam," Mr. Wells chuckles, "our spy *was* the Saint Bernard."

My jaw drops. "Huh?"

"The tailor I had summoned to the embassy was actually the costume designer for a famous theatrical troupe in that city. He smuggled in yards of synthetic fur as well as bottles of dye and jars of paint. He even managed to conceal a box of glass eyeballs. Once he arrived at the embassy, he set about sewing and painting and clipping the furry fabric until he had created a Saint Bernard suit, complete with a mouth that opened and eyes that blinked."

"No way!" I gasp.

"Way! And while the tailor was building the costume, I had our technical staff record the growls and barks of the ambassador's dogs. We transferred those sounds onto a playback device that was controlled from inside the dog suit and connected by wire to mini speakers hidden inside the wooden kennel."

"So what did the soldiers think when you returned without a dog in your truck?"

"Oh, we had anticipated that," Mr. Wells says. "After leaving the border, I drove to the cargo hangar at the local airfield, where I picked up two Saint Bernard puppies that the ambassador had just purchased from a breeder in Switzerland. When I returned to the embassy, the soldiers, of course, crowded around the crate to look at the cute newborns."

"Didn't they wonder where the puppies' mother was?"

Mr. Wells nods. "When they asked, I lowered my chin and shook my head sadly. And do you know? Every one of those enemy soldiers bowed his head, pulled off his cap and observed a moment of silence for that poor, departed dog."

"Wow." I sigh. "When I grow up, I want your job."

"There is one final chapter to the story," Mr. Wells says. "As a favor to the tailor for his invaluable help, I arranged to smuggle him, his wife and their little boy out of that war-torn country and into Japan, where I supplied them with passports and a new family name."

"That was a pretty nice favor," I say.

"Perhaps," he says with a shrug, "but that tailor's little boy grew up, entered the field of medicine and has more than adequately repaid my favor over the years."

He turns and nods to Dr. Sakata, who makes a deep bow in return.

THE BAD NEWS OF BOOKKEEPING
December 31–January 1

The sixth day of Christmas is December 31, the last day of the year. As if to remind us of what a rotten year it's been, the weather is especially lousy. A cold rain has been falling for hours by the time Dad is ready to leave for the bakery.

"I don't know why I'm even bothering," he grumbles as he slips his coat on. "Nobody's going to be out buying cupcakes in this weather."

When I get to work, Dr. Sakata leads me into the first-floor office, where Mr. Wells is studying the map of Bay Front that I marked up the day before. I move toward the chair opposite him, but Mr. Wells suddenly looks up. "Don't sit," he orders. "We have another job to do."

Hoko pads along behind us as Dr. Sakata pushes Mr. Wells's wheelchair out of the office and down to the end of a hallway I've never been in. We stop in front of a carved oak door, and Dr. Sakata presses a button that's hidden in the dark wood molding. Instead of swinging open, though, the door slides away to reveal—

"An elevator?" I gasp. "You've got an elevator?"

"The house came with it," Mr. Wells explains as he rolls in. "Normally, I take the stairs to stay in shape, but it sure comes in handy now that I'm in this chair."

We descend to the basement and make our way to the large workroom where Dr. Sakata and Mr. Wells had loaded the money into all those items I'd bought for the Red Mission. Again, fifteen one-hundred-dollar bills are arranged down the middle of the steel worktable. The marble chop with the carving of the phoenix and the bottle of purple ink are carefully laid out, too.

As he pulls on a pair of white cotton gloves, Mr. Wells says, "I thought that it was time you acquire another of the many skills in Nickel Bay Nick's arsenal."

"What skill is that?"

"The preparation of the money," he says, holding out a smaller pair of gloves to me.

I'm surprised. "You got gloves in my size?"

"An operative is only as good as his equipment." Mr. Wells rolls up the sleeves of his sweater and gets down to business.

First, he explains, I have to learn the proper technique of inking the chop. Too much ink and the image smudges. Too little ink and the image is faint. Once the stamp is properly inked, Mr. Wells demonstrates how to apply it—with one smooth rolling motion. He sits at my elbow as I practice stamping thirty or forty small squares of scrap paper. Then, with the magnifying eyeglasses strapped to his forehead, Mr. Wells inspects each one as carefully as if he were examining a cut diamond. Finally satisfied, he declares, "I think we can move on to the real thing."

He nods to Dr. Sakata, who gathers up my test pages, piles them in a corner fireplace and sets fire to them. All of us, including Hoko, watch the flames consume the papers until all that's left of my practice sheets is a smoking pile of black ash. Then slowly, carefully and—if I do say so myself—expertly, I stamp fifteen purple phoenixes onto fifteen crisp hundred-dollar bills.

Over lunch, Mr. Wells is all business. "The next time we see each other will be Wednesday, January second. Be here at one o'clock. You and Dr. Sakata can continue your pickpocketing exercises, and then, just before sunset, you'll take the cash and leave for Bay Front. By the time you walk across town, it'll be dark, and you can begin the Green Mission."

In the middle of the afternoon, Mr. Wells calls Dad at the bakery. He starts the conversation by going on and on about how impressed he is by my filing skills and how "invaluable" my help has been. Once he's got Dad all buttered up, he makes his request.

"So, Dwight, listen. I've got a favor to ask. The day after tomorrow . . . yes, Wednesday . . . I've got an appointment that's going to take me out of the house all morning.
Sam and I have been working at such a good clip that I'd
hate to lose eight hours of work, especially with tomorrow being a holiday and all."

From where I'm sitting, I can hear Dad through the
phone exclaiming, "No, no! Of course not."

"So what I'm hoping," Mr. Wells continues smoothly,
"is that Sam can start work that afternoon—say, about
one?—and we'll knock off at about nine. Is that okay with
you?"

I don't have to hear his exact words to know that Dad is
thrilled to have an evening to himself. And Lisa, probably.

Mr. Wells hangs up and says, "I like your father."

"Try living with him," I grumble.

"Why is that so hard?"

"Where do I start?" I ask. "First of all, he expects me to
be perfect, like him. And I'm not."

"You think your father is perfect?"

"He was a state champion football player!" I exclaim.
"He was a fireman who saved lives! And what am I? A
pasty-white, scrawny punk made out of spare parts. And
all I ever do is disappoint him."

"Is that how *he* feels?" Mr. Wells says quietly. "Has he
said that you're a disappointment to him?"

I look away before I answer, "He doesn't have to."

"Well, before you beat yourself up," he says, "perhaps you should ask the question."

Hoko sleeps in a corner and snores loudly through the next three hours of my frustrating pickpocketing lesson with Dr. Sakata. At the end of the afternoon, I gloomily pull on my sweater and shoes at the back door. As I reach for the knob, Mr. Wells stops me. "Aren't you forgetting something?" he asks.

I turn to find him, Dr. Sakata and Hoko lined up.

"What?"

"Happy New Year, Sam," Mr. Wells says with a little nod, and Dr. Sakata bows and says something in his language. Hoko simply yawns.

"Oh, yeah." I sort of nod, sort of bow. "Happy New Year, you guys."

After he gets home from work, Dad showers before getting dressed for Lisa's New Year's party. When I walk out in ripped blue jeans, he shakes his head.

"You're not wearing those."

"Apparently I am."

He sighs. "Don't be difficult, Sam."

"I'm not being difficult," I insist. "I'm being comfortable. If I'm going to have to go to a party that I don't want to go to, at least let me wear what I want to wear."

Dad folds his arms. "Is this about Lisa?"

"What?"

"Has Lisa ever done anything to make you dislike her?"

"No! But—"

"Have you got a problem with me seeing Lisa?"

"You can see whoever you—"

"Answer the question: Are you upset that I'm dating someone who isn't your mother?"

"Mom got remarried!" I spit out. "Or did you forget?"

"How could I forget?" Dad shouts, throwing his hands up. "I think about her every day."

That hits me like a sucker punch. "You do?"

"Sam," Dad says gently, "your mother was my high school sweetheart. We started a family together. When she left, she broke my heart." His voice cracks a little on that last part.

Outside, the last winds of the year rattle through the eaves as Dad and I face each other, neither one moving. Finally I groan. "All right." I trudge into my bedroom, announcing, "I'll find something uncomfortable to wear."

Surprise, surprise. Lisa's party doesn't suck.

"You look very nice tonight, Sam," she says as she welcomes me with a hug.

"Thanks," I say. "You, too." And I mean it. Lisa's wearing a dark green velvet dress that looks good with her curly red hair, and when Dad kisses her hello, her smile lights up the room.

Lisa's small apartment is crammed with people in a holiday mood, drinking happily and loading their plates from the platters of food on the dining room table. There are some other kids there, so Lisa's two little girls have enough playmates that they leave me alone. I pour myself a cup of the eggnog ("From the nonalcoholic punchbowl," Dad warns), and I wander around, eavesdropping on conversations. And guess what they're all talking about?

Nickel Bay Nick.

I stand behind a bald guy who's suspicious that the latest visit was pulled off by a fake. "Think about it," he says. "Nickel Bay Nick has never waited until after Christmas before."

Others wonder when Nick will strike again. Or whether he *will* strike again.

Just wait! I want to shout. *Wait till Wednesday!* But, like any good operative, I keep my mouth shut.

What's causing the most buzz is the news that some microchip company has decided to build its new factory in town. "I was giving the president of Micro-Marvel a tour of Nickel Bay," a well-dressed woman is saying, "and it happened to be the very day that Nick made his return. Well!" She throws her head back and laughs. "When Mr. Micro-Marvel saw our citizens literally dancing in the streets, he decided right then and there that Nickel Bay is the *perfect* community for his new facility."

All around her, people jabber excitedly. "Isn't that amazing, Sam?" Lisa asks when she sees me. "All those new jobs?"

"I guess," I mumble, and fade back into the crowd, afraid that even a tiny, proud smile might betray my secret identity.

Much later I'm sitting on the pile of coats on Lisa's bed, watching the ball drop in Times Square on TV, when I hear the countdown start out in the living room. "Three . . . two . . . one . . . HAPPY NEW YEAR!" shout fifty or sixty voices, followed by laughter and the sound of glasses clinking.

"There you are."

I look up, and Dad's in the doorway.

"Am I not supposed to be in here?" I ask.

"No, you're fine, Sam," he says. "Just wanted to wish you a Happy New Year."

I get the feeling he wants a hug, but that hug we shared at Town Hall was way more hugging than I'm used to.

"Yeah," I mutter, and fold my arms across my chest. "You, too."

He starts to go, but I stop him by saying, "You know I'm never going to be a football star, right?"

He turns and looks at me for a long time before he answers. "Football stars are a dime a dozen. You, Sam . . . you're one in a million."

He's never said that before.

Despite the lump in my throat, I manage to say, "Thanks."

When my alarm goes off the next morning at seven thirty, I half sleepwalk to the bathroom and take my pill, but then I go right back to bed and wake up at about noon. By the time I shuffle into the kitchen, scratching and yawning, Dad is already deep into his bookkeeping.

It may be New Year's Day for the rest of the world, but for Dad, it's the day he does the Nickel Bay Bakery and Cupcakery's year-end accounting. I know better than to try to speak to him as he punches numbers into the calculator and works his way through the piles of receipts and stacks of bills covering the kitchen table. After eating my Cap'n Crunch standing over the sink, I take a shower.

As the afternoon drags on, I miss my routine with Mr. Wells and Dr. Sakata. I even miss Hoko. Since Dad took my video games away, restricted use of the computer to school nights and canceled the Internet because it costs too much, I don't have anything to do. Every TV channel is showing football, but none of my teams are playing, so I am truly, totally bored.

When I announce, "I'm gonna call Jaxon, okay?" Dad grunts, "Fine." But Jaxon's at some fancy country club with his lawyer father and the rest of his family, so he can't get away to hang out.

I think about calling Ivy. I've never had the nerve to

speak to her without Jaxon around, but when I remind myself that I *am* Nickel Bay Nick, I somehow find the courage to dial her number. The call goes to voice mail, and I almost hang up, but at the last second I take the plunge.

"Yeah. Hi, Ivy. It's me. And by 'me,' I mean Sam," I stammer. "Just calling to say 'Happy New Year.' Cuz it's New Year's Day, right? So . . . be happy, okay?" As the words leave my lips, they sound so amazingly stupid that I wish I could reach into the phone and pull them back. I squeeze my eyes shut and mutter, "Stop talking, Sam." But when I suddenly remember that I'm still connected, I shout, "That's all! Bye!" and snap the phone shut. Then I use it to whack myself on the forehead.

How dumb did I just sound? I ask myself over and over.

For about five minutes I consider calling back to say, "Ivy? *Please* ignore my previous message," but I'm sure I'd only get tongue-tied all over again. My brain keeps replaying my humiliating blunder until I pass the kitchen and see Dad. His back is to me, and he's holding his head in his hands.

"Dad?" I say softly. "Everything okay?"

He lifts his head and blows his nose in a paper towel. Without turning, he says, "I don't know, Sam. I don't know."

And just like that, the sinking feeling I got after leaving Ivy's message disappears, and I start to worry about what's making my dad cry.

I lie in bed later, thinking about all the happy, hopeful faces at Lisa's party. Was that really less than twenty-four hours ago? I remember feeling so excited because, by being Nickel Bay Nick, I had given a new sense of hope to everyone in the room.

Everyone, it turns out, except my own father.

Off and on through the night, I come half awake. Every time I do, I can see the glow from the kitchen light still bouncing off my bedroom ceiling, and I know Dad's still working. Finally I drop off into a deep sleep and dream of me and him and Mom, laughing and running through the spray of a lawn sprinkler, just like we used to do on hot summer days when I was three.

THE CLOSE CALL BY THE BAY

January 2

The second of January starts with about six inches of snow on the ground. By the time I take my morning pill, though, the sun is starting to break through, and the icicles along our roofline are dripping steadily. Dad has cleared the kitchen table of all his bookkeeping stuff, and except for the dark circles under his eyes that tell me he didn't get much sleep, there's no trace of yesterday's ordeal.

On his way out, Dad struggles with the cardboard box full of his checkbooks and receipts. I reach around and open the front door for him as I ask, "You remember I'm working late tonight, right?"

"I do," he says as he starts down the stairs to his car. "But I'm still going to call you at seven thirty."

I've got hours to kill before going to work, and after thirty minutes, I'm desperate for a distraction. Then I remember that I still haven't gotten anywhere with my investigation of Mr. Wells. He's hiding something. I feel it in my bones. If I could only figure out what it is, I bet I could blow his mind the way he blew mine when he showed me all my police files.

Suddenly, the sound of a garbage truck outside in the alley gives me an idea.

If I could go through Mr. Wells's trash, who knows what I might find? A membership card from a secret club he belongs to? Maybe a letter from an old spy buddy? Or even a Christmas card from a king?

I yank my shoes on, pull a sweater over my head and grab my jacket as I dash out the door and down the stairs. But by the time I slip into the alley through the back fence and race around the corner, the garbage truck is already pulling away from the trash cans outside Mr. Wells's backyard fence and turning onto Sherwood Avenue.

"Rats!" I grumble, kicking at a clump of snow. "That was a really good idea."

As long as I'm dressed and out of the house, though, I figure I might as well continue my investigation. The Nickel Bay Public Library offers free Wi-Fi service, so I head over there, planning to do an Internet search for Mr. Herbert Wells.

On my way, I can't help but notice how great Nickel Bay is looking under the perfectly blue sky. Runoff from melting snow is gurgling down the gutters as people shovel their walks and kids hurl snowballs at each other. A street crew is patching potholes on Griffin Drive, and a couple guys on a crane are repairing the WALK/DON'T WALK sign that's been flickering for six months at one corner of Brownlow Square.

I'm starting up the library steps when somebody calls my name, and I turn to see Ivy waving from in front of a dry cleaner's across the street. She's with her mom, who continues into the store as Ivy runs over to me.

"Hey, Ivy," I say. "Howzit goin'?"

"I got your message," she says, and I can feel the blood rush to my face.

"That was so lame," I start to explain. "'Be happy' and all that . . ."

"No! It wasn't lame," she insists. "I thought it was sweet."

"Whatever."

"I'm sorry I didn't call back," she explains, "but I had the most amazing day. My uncle's a science professor at the college. So yesterday, when there was nobody on campus, he took me into one of his laboratories, and we did experiments all afternoon. With chemicals and electricity and stuff."

"That's so cool," I say. "You're totally gonna be a scientist someday. I just know it."

"I hope," she says, and then there's a long pause, until she asks, "Sam? Did we hurt your feelings the day Jaxon made fun of you for buying that hair dye?"

"Hurt my feelings?" I force a laugh. "Ha! What're you talking about?"

"You looked kind of upset. And the next night you wouldn't go downtown with us . . . ?"

"I didn't have any money," I remind her.

"Oh." She digs the toe of one shoe into a library step, and after a moment says, "Look, I know how Jaxon can be sometimes. Lately, y'know? Just because I have to give myself injections for my diabetes, he's started calling me Pincushion."

"That sucks," I say. "You can't let him do that, if it bothers you."

"I know, right? Can I tell you something?" she asks, and I nod. "Most of the stuff Jaxon suggests, I only do it because I get the feeling you want to."

"Me?" I sputter. "I only go along because *you* do."

"Well, is that dumb or what?" Ivy says with a laugh.

"I guess it is, huh?" And then I crack up, too.

After our laughter dies down, Ivy speaks. "We've got to stand up for ourselves, Sam. We can't let Jaxon boss us around anymore." She extends a hand. "Deal?"

I take her hand, but the feel of Ivy's skin knocks every word out of my head. It's only when she says, "Promise me, Sam," that I'm able to mutter, "Okay, okay," before letting go.

Ivy smiles and pulls a strand of hair over one ear. "You know, he and I are going on to the high school next year."

My mind's still reeling when I answer, "So?"

163

"I'm just sayin', maybe it's time you ought to think about making some new friends."

"That's not so easy."

"C'mon, Sam," she prods. "You're smart. You're funny."

"I'm not funny." I scrunch up my nose. "Am I?"

She giggles. "When you make faces like that, you totally are!"

I blush and look away just as Ivy's mom calls from across the street. "Gotta go," she says, but before running off—and I'm not making this up!—she kisses me on the cheek. "And, Sam?" she says as she runs off. "Happy New Year!"

For a long time I stand in that one spot, replaying our conversation in my head. We've never had a private talk, so until that moment, I never knew how Ivy felt about Jaxon's stunts. And if I hadn't left her that dorky phone message, I'd never have known. I touch the spot where her lips met my cheek, and a warm glow spreads through me.

When I finally shake off my daze, I check my watch and discover that I've got to get to work. Because Ivy distracted me, my investigation into Mr. Wells's secrets will have to wait.

But the distraction was worth it.

After another disastrous put-pocket training session that lasts through the early afternoon, Mr. Wells suggests we take a break. Dr. Sakata makes a pot of peppermint tea, which he serves in steaming mugs at the kitchen table, along with a plate of amazing gingerbread squares. He may be an intimidating hulk, but Dr. Sakata sure knows his way around a cookie sheet.

When we're nearly finished, Mr. Wells calls out, "Hoko!" followed by something in that foreign language, and Hoko immediately runs out of the room.

"Is that Japanese, what you said to him?" I ask.

"It is. Hoko is a chow chow. It's an Asian breed."

"So he doesn't understand English?"

"Hoko?" Mr. Wells gives a little laugh and says something to Dr. Sakata, who chuckles, too. "With Dr. Sakata in the house, we both address Hoko in Japanese. But Hoko is also familiar with English, Korean, some Spanish and a little German," he explains. "He's a well-traveled dog."

"Wow," I mutter. "All I can say is 'bite me' in Polish."

Hoko trots back into the kitchen, gripping the handle of a large shopping bag in his teeth. Instead of delivering it to Mr. Wells, though, he crosses and sits next to my chair.

"He thinks it's for me," I say.

"He is correct."

"Seriously?" I look back and forth between him and Hoko. "He's not going to take a chunk out of me?" Mr. Wells shakes his head. Very slowly, I take hold of the bag's handle, and Hoko eases his jaws apart. "What's this?"

"Open it."

All the clothes in the bag are black. Black jeans. Black long johns. Black sweatshirt. Black coat, black socks and black sneakers. All in my size.

"Your wardrobe for tonight's job," Mr. Wells explains. "You can put those on before you leave here, and when Dr. Sakata returns you afterward, you'll change back into your own clothes before going home."

When I come out of a small bathroom, dressed from head to toe in black, I spread my arms and say, "I look like a ninja."

"You have a lot in common with ninjas." Mr. Wells circles me in his wheelchair. "Did you know that as far back as fourteenth-century Japan, ninjas were spies and undercover soldiers who deliberately disguised themselves to perform feats of espionage and sabotage?"

"Really?" I scratch my head. "I've only seen them in video games. And movies."

Mr. Wells puts on his white cotton gloves before handing me the stack of bills and showing me a pocket inside my new black coat that's the perfect place to store them.

"Sunset will be at four fifty-three this afternoon." he says, and we both check our watches.

"Four minutes from now," I confirm.

"By the time you walk to Bay Front," he says, "it should be totally dark. On your way, then."

I feel like I should get a salute or at least a handshake.

Instead, Mr. Wells rolls away, calling back over one shoulder, "Stay low to the ground."

The light is already fading when I let myself out the backyard gate by punching in *oh-one-oh-five*. Just before I exit the alley onto Sherwood Avenue, I see Crummer Sikes's Animal Control van coming, and I duck behind a telephone pole. He's already seen me in the alley once before, and I don't want to make it a habit. He rolls past, looking this way and that, but he doesn't spot me. Once he's gone, I pull my black knit cap low over my ears and point my black sneakers in the direction of Bay Front Drive.

On my way, I mentally review the tips Mr. Wells gave me for spotting unlocked cars. Sloppy people, I remember him saying, don't lock their cars as often as neat people, so I should be on the lookout for cluttered front seats and messy dashboards.

The longer someone owns a vehicle, he taught me, the more unlikely they are to lock it, so I'm supposed to look for old cars.

"And keep an eye out for funny bumper stickers," he advised. "People who glue announcements like HONK IF YOU LOVE BEER to their fenders don't tend to worry about security."

My route winds through side streets and back alleys, and eventually I find myself behind the building where the Nickel Bay Bakery and Cupcakery is located. For the heck of it, I walk to the front and sneak a peek into Dad's store.

He's in there with a single customer. A stooped old lady in a cloth coat is pointing to the cupcakes in the display case, and I bet she's asking about every flavor in there. Like he always does, Dad will patiently explain all eight varieties on display, and then, I'm sure, the lady will end up buying only one or two.

But I don't have the time to hang around and see if I'm right. I've got a job to do.

By the time I get to Bay Front, it's dark. About half the neon signs on the boulevard are unlit where restaurants are no longer in business, but the rest of the signs sizzle and glow against the black sky. Lucky for me, there's hardly any moonlight tonight.

I huddle behind the base of a burnt-out streetlamp and watch people arriving for happy hour or dinner. I note where they park and which restaurants they enter. Despite the earlier snowfall, the day warmed up and now, even with puffs of wind coming off the bay, the evening is pretty mild. Because of that, I notice, people are a lot more casual about not rolling up their windows or locking their doors. After studying the street for over an hour, I pick out four or five cars that I know I'll have no trouble getting into, hum a few bars of "I'm So Ready," and begin the Green Mission.

By wriggling my skinny arm through a half-opened window of a rusty, old Mustang, I'm able to fold a Nickel Bay Ben over the steering wheel where only the driver will see it. Across the street, there's a pickup truck with a bumper sticker that reads BUCKLE UP. IT MAKES IT HARDER FOR THE ALIENS TO SUCK YOU OUT OF YOUR CAR. Just like Mr. Wells predicted, its doors are unlocked, so I slip a Ben in between the radio buttons.

Dressed completely in black, I feel practically invisible. When I see someone coming, I squeeze into a doorway or crouch into a tight ball between parked cars, holding my breath until they pass by. Then I spring back into action. Slinking in the shadows, I weave back and forth across Bay Front Drive and up a few side streets, hitting one vehicle after another. I work my way down the waterfront until, about forty-five minutes later, I arrive at Pirro's Pasta Palace, where I get an unpleasant surprise.

A tall, skinny guy is on valet duty. The afternoon I did my scouting and laid out my route, there was nobody parking cars here. I sure don't want a witness tonight!

My first impulse is to skip the place altogether. What if this guy sees me? What if I open a car door and a chime dings or an interior light goes on? But then I realize there are a lot of cars in there, and I have to unload a few more Bens. I'm not giving up so easily.

Squatting behind a mailbox across the street, I notice that, after the attendant parks each car at the back of

Pirro's dimly lit lot, he doesn't bother to lock it before returning to his valet stand at the front. So once a taxi cruises by, I dash across Bay Front Drive, circle the block, sneak down an alley and enter the back of Pirro's parking area, where I wait for a few new customers to arrive. Then, in the time it takes for the valet to open each driver's door and hand them a parking stub, I make my drops.

One goes into the glove compartment of a Toyota compact.

A few spots over, I place the final Nickel Bay Buck in a Chevy truck.

And then it happens.

My cell phone rings. I drop to the pavement like I've been shot, but not before I see the valet's head snap in my direction. Did he see me?

Running footsteps crunch across the parking lot gravel.

Yup, he saw me.

Fumbling, I flip open the phone to stop it from ringing. "Did you take your pill?" Dad asks.

"Yeah, yeah, yeah," I whisper desperately. With my cheek pressed against the gravel, I can see between tires to where—four or five spaces away—a pair of feet race back and forth.

"Why are you whispering?" Dad wants to know.

"Uh . . . Mr. Wells is concentrating," I hiss. "Okay, gotta go."

Before I can hang up, though, the valet shouts, "Who's there?" and Dad asks, "Who's that?"

"Who's who?" I reply. I don't dare hang up. Dad will only call back.

"Who's that yelling?" Dad asks.

"It's . . . it's the TV," I stutter.

"If Mr. Wells is concentrating, why does he have the TV on?"

"Good question," I answer. "I'll ask him. Bye!" I gently close the phone. The valet is one car away, so close that I can see that he's wearing white socks with black dress shoes.

"Don't think I didn't see you!" He yells into the night. "I saw you!" With two more steps, he'll round the corner and find me on the ground, so I tuck in my arms, roll *under* the SUV and watch, breathless, as he steps into the very spot I had occupied two seconds before.

Keep walking! I plead silently. *Please keep walking!*

But the shoes stop. Back up a step. Then, to my horror, a knee lowers to the pavement. Then another. In the next split second, he'll peer under the car, and the Green Mission will be all over!

At that exact moment, headlights sweep the lot. A driver pulls in from Bay Front Drive and toots his horn impatiently. "Be right there!" the valet shouts, springing to his feet and sprinting toward the parking lot entrance.

In a flash, I roll out from my hiding place and scramble up to a crouch. Like a black ninja duck, I waddle into the alley behind Pirro's and dash a full city block before I stagger up against a Dumpster. As I gasp for breath, I'm suddenly aware of horns honking. On tiptoe, I slink between buildings and peek down Bay Front Drive.

At the other end of the street, back where I began making drops over an hour before, I hear people hooting and hollering in celebration. By squinting, I can see them flashing their headlights and even dancing in traffic. For a moment, I let myself enjoy the spectacle of adults acting like kids on Christmas morning, but the spell is broken when a police cruiser, sirens wailing and lights flashing, squeals past me and skids to a halt in front of Pirro's Pasta Palace. Two patrolmen—Officer Brockman and Officer Ferguson—jump out of their squad car, and they're met by the valet, who's rattling away at about a hundred miles an hour and gesturing wildly toward his lot. The cops pull flashlights from their holsters and follow him.

Inside my chest, my heart is still beating so hard it actually aches. I'm only a half block from where I'm supposed to rendezvous with Dr. Sakata, so I pull out my phone and autodial Mr. Wells. After one ring, he answers and simply barks, "He's on his way," before hanging up.

I snort at the phone. "That's it?" I mutter. "'*He's on his way*'? No 'How'd things go?' or 'You okay?'"

The sounds of merriment move down Bay Front as more people along my route discover Nickel Bay Bens. *I wish that Mr. Wells were here to hear this,* I find myself thinking. Maybe then he'd appreciate what I've done and wouldn't treat me like such a schmo. I pace, trying to stay warm now that I'm no longer on the move. I work up a mouthful of saliva to swallow my seven-thirty pill, but when I reach into my jacket pocket for it, I'm horrified to discover one last Nickel Bay Buck. I thought I'd gotten rid of them, but in all the excitement, I guess I lost count.

Great! Just great! I can only imagine what's gonna happen when I return without distributing every last Benjamin we stamped. Mr. Wells, I'll bet, is gonna sigh and roll his eyes. He'll exchange looks with Dr. Sakata and they'll both shake their heads, disappointed by my unfinished mission.

I'm not going to give them that satisfaction.

The flashing lights from the police car are sweeping the street as I poke my head around the corner, searching for one final drop. Within a block I can see a Honda Accord, a Chevy Silverado and a BMW. Not one of them looks like an easy mark.

When I see the police cruiser, though, I flash back to all the times I've found myself caged in the backseat of one, and you know what I remember? Whenever officers pull up to a crime scene and jump out, they never stop to lock their doors or set an alarm. Why would they? *Who's gonna steal a cop car?*

Giggling, I scamper across the street and ease open the driver's door of the NBPD cruiser. Leaning across the front seat, I stick my final Ben in the handset of the two-way radio.

Green Mission accomplished!

I run the last half block to the abandoned church, where Dr. Sakata is idling in the SUV with the headlights off. The second I jump in and shut the door, Dr. Sakata whips a U-turn and glides up a side street, away from all the celebrating down on Bay Front Drive.

Without a word, he hands me a thermos, which happens to be filled with hot mint tea. I pour a cup and take my seven-thirty pill. "Thank! You!" I say loudly and distinctly to Dr. Sakata, who simply nods.

Although I'm still trembling a little from the scare I got in Pirro's parking lot, I once again find myself feeling the way I did at the end of the Red Mission.

No shouts of triumph.

No backslapping or high-fiving.

Being a hero, I guess, is a quiet thing.

"How'd it go?" Mr. Wells wheels out of his office to meet us the second we walk in.

"Just as we planned," I say coolly. "That's why it's called a plan."

"Fifteen bills, fifteen drops?"

I nod. "Check."

Mr. Wells notices the mud and gravel on my pants and jacket. "Spent a little time on the ground, did you?"

"There was one close call," I admit, "but nobody saw me."

"Good." He jerks his head toward his office, from which I can hear the sound of a television. "The local stations have interrupted their regular programming to broadcast live from Bay Front Drive. There are a lot of happy people down there tonight."

"I'll watch when I get home," I say. "Right now I just want to get out of this ninja gear."

After I change, I carry my clothes into the kitchen, where Mr. Wells and Dr. Sakata are sipping tea while watching reports of Nickel Bay Nick's latest visit on the countertop TV.

"Where should I put these?" I ask.

Mr. Wells mutes the TV and turns to me. "Set them down there." He points to an empty countertop. "Dr. Sakata will dispose of those."

I dump the clothes, brush my hands off and zip up my jacket. "Same time tomorrow morning?"

"Same time." Mr. Wells nods. I turn to exit by the back door when Mr. Wells stops me with, "And, Sam?"

I spin around. "Yeah?"

"From what I can tell," he says, "you wrote a new chapter in the history of Nickel Bay Nick this evening. Well done."

His compliment catches me by surprise.

"Uh . . . thanks." I shrug. Nobody knows what to say next, but then Hoko sneezes, and that breaks the awkward silence.

I pull on my gloves and mumble, "See ya," before I head out.

Walking home down the back alley, an unexpected

thought pops into my head. Unlike the Red Mission, in which Mr. Wells laid out every single move I was expected to make, I had plotted my own journey down Bay Front Drive. I had chosen my hiding places. I had selected the cars I would hit. *That was all me tonight,* I realize. *I did that.*

Even with Jaxon and Ivy, it's never been that way. Every job we've ever pulled, all the trouble we get into together—it's always Jaxon's idea. I go along, like I don't have a mind of my own. But tonight, I felt . . . capable. Skillful. Talented, even.

Once I get home and slip into my sweatpants, I'm suddenly dog-tired. All the nervous excitement of the Green Mission catches up with me, and I fall asleep standing at the bathroom sink while brushing my teeth. It's only when the front door closes behind Dad as he tiptoes in from his date with Lisa that I jolt awake and find toothpaste hanging from my chin in one long drool. I quickly rinse and spit before Dad pops his head in to say, "Hey, kiddo, did you hear? Nickel Bay Nick paid a visit to Bay Front tonight."

"Saw it on TV," I mutter, eyes half shut, as I stumble past him into my bedroom, where I fall face-first into my pillow.

THE **PLACE I'M NOT WELCOME**

January 3

"You were seen last night," Mr. Wells says the next morning in place of a greeting.

"What?" I ask quickly. "Who saw me?"

"I taped this from the morning news." Mr. Wells points a remote control at a wide-screen TV on the office wall and the screen lights up with the image of . . .

"The valet!" I gasp. "That's the guy who parks cars at Pirro's Pasta Palace."

"He's suddenly famous." Instead of sounding angry, Mr. Wells seems amused. "Apparently he's the only eyewitness to Nick's visit."

In the daylight, I can see that the guy is barely out of his teens. He seems very excited to be on camera, as he practically shouts into the reporter's microphone, "I thought it was a carjacker. But then everybody started findin' that special money, and, man! I'm tellin' you! Nickel Bay Nick was in my lot!"

"And can you tell us what he looked like?" asks the interviewer.

"Okay, well . . . he wasn't real tall," the valet starts to answer.

I turn to Mr. Wells and grimace. "What if he describes me?"

"Just watch," Mr. Wells replies.

"But he wasn't short, either," the valet continues.

"Did you get a hair color?" asks the reporter.

"Black. Black and long. Or brown, maybe."

"Did you see his face?"

"He had a beard. Definitely a beard. I think." Then the guy explodes. "Heck, I don't know! It was dark! All I can tell you for sure is that I was this close"—he holds his hands two feet apart—"*this* close to grabbing Nickel Bay Nick."

I exhale in relief. "In other words, he doesn't have a clue."

Mr. Wells snaps off the TV and hands the remote to Dr. Sakata. "Our secret is still safe." He picks up the morning paper. "And have you seen this?" On the front page of the *Nickel Bay News,* under the headline NICKEL BAY NICK STRIKES AGAIN!!! are about a dozen photos of happy people who, after dining out last night, returned to their cars to find that they had been . . . visited.

"Today is the ninth day of Christmas, and the media has apparently been doing their math," Mr. Wells says.

"What does that mean?"

"They've figured out that last night's drop was four days since Nick's first appearance, so it would seem that I . . . or, rather, you . . . are back on Nick's schedule."

"So they'll be expecting the final mission four days from yesterday."

"This Sunday. Correct. But they don't know where."

"Neither do I," I point out.

"And that's our work for today."

Dr. Sakata, Hoko and I follow as Mr. Wells rolls out of the living room. "It should come as no surprise that the White Mission requires you to move among crowds of shoppers and slip money into their jackets and purses."

"You mean put-pocketing."

"Exactly."

"But my lessons with Dr. Sakata have been total disasters," I remind him.

"True." Mr. Wells nods. "Your put-pocketing skills are nowhere nearly as refined as I would like. *Yet.* But we still have three days, and we'll need every precious minute." As we enter his office, Mr. Wells says, "The excitement generated by Nickel Bay Nick's first two strikes has resulted in an amazing post-Christmas boom at businesses all over town, which is all very gratifying." He turns to me. "But it's also a little scary."

"Why 'scary'?"

"Because it means that wherever we choose to carry

out Sunday's White Mission, crowds will be at record levels," he explains. "The good news is that more people provide you with more cover. The bad news is that most of those people will be hoping to get a look at Nickel Bay Nick. Instead of sneaking about under cover of darkness, you will now be operating in broad daylight. In full view of thousands of people."

His words make my stomach flutter. "You make it sound dangerous."

"It *is* dangerous. Operation Christmas Rescue—and the entire legacy of Nickel Bay Nick—depends on your flawless execution of the White Mission." He stops rolling. "Taking all of these variables into consideration, I have decided that you'll execute the White Mission . . . here." He sweeps an arm to the bulletin board, where a full-color foldout map is thumbtacked, and when I see the diagram posted there, the blood drains from my face.

"That's . . . the Four Corners Mall," I stammer.

"Precisely."

The Four Corners Mall is a big, five-story shopping arcade, built on what used to be swampland out near the border of Nickel Bay County.

"But . . . I'm not allowed in there!" I say.

He spins his wheelchair around. "I know."

"You *know*?!" I yelp.

Mr. Wells folds his hands in his lap. "Take a deep breath."

"But . . . but . . . !" I can't even make a sentence.

"Breathe!" he orders.

So I do.

"Now, Sam. I know from your files that you are . . . how should I put this? . . . *unwelcome* at the Four Corners."

"*Unwelcome?*" I cry. "I'm banned for life!"

"So it says in the police report," Mr. Wells says, "but the details are sketchy. Why don't you fill me in?"

So I tell him about all the stores and stalls at the Four Corners Mall where Jaxon and Ivy and I used to shoplift. I tell him about the clerks and mall cops who'd chase after us as we'd run the wrong way down escalators or split off in three separate directions. "And then one day," I explain, "we go into JC Penney to pick up a few items—"

"And by 'pick up a few items,'" Mr. Wells interrupts, "you mean . . ."

"I mean exactly what you think I mean."

Mr. Wells nods. "Go on."

"As soon as we walk in the store, these two security guards start tailing us, and they don't stop. Finally, we get so nervous, we leave without taking a single thing we'd come for. But we were mad. I mean, we hadn't even done anything!"

"Apparently, your reputations preceded you."

"What does that mean?"

"It means that people had come to expect a certain kind of behavior from you three."

"Well, yeah, maybe that. Anyway, we decide we want revenge on JC Penney, so we split up and sneak into the store later that same day. And between the three of us, we're carrying a dozen eggs in our jacket pockets."

"Raw eggs?"

"Fresh off the shelf."

"Did you steal those, too?"

"What do you think?"

Mr. Wells purses his lips, and I continue. "Each of us goes into a clothing department—men's, women's, children's—and we slip those eggs down into the folds of sweaters or whatever clothes are stacked up on the counters and tables. Then we hide behind the mannequins and watch what happens."

"Let me guess," Mr. Wells says. "An unsuspecting shopper wanders by, sees an interesting item of clothing, picks it up and shakes it out to examine it . . ."

"And then *splat!*" I laugh. "From where we're hiding, we can hear eggs falling all over the store. And there's people yelling, 'Oh, no!' And not just 'Oh, no!' but a lot of other words that people shouldn't yell in public."

"You sound proud of what you did."

"At the time, yeah!" I chuckle. "We thought we were being hard-core. Getting revenge, y'know?"

"And now?"

"Now?"

"Sam," he says, "you've been Nickel Bay Nick for eight days. You've brought joy and hope to an entire town. You've lifted the spirits of thousands of people. How do you feel now about getting revenge by cracking raw eggs in the aisles of a department store?"

My scalp burns with embarrassment. Mr. Wells lets his words hang in the air long enough to make me squirm, before he says, "And that's when you were caught on tape?"

"Jaxon and Ivy hid their faces, but stupid me! They got me on surveillance camera," I grumble. "After that, the guards at every entrance to the mall were given my picture and told to stop me on sight. I haven't been back since."

"And that is why," Mr. Wells says, "we're going to have you go in disguise. Or, I should say, *disguises.*"

"You mean, like, a few?"

"At least a few," he says. "But we'll deal with your wardrobe tomorrow. Today we're going to perform a complete inspection of the Four Corners Mall."

"How?" I moan. "I told you I can't walk in the place."

"Which is why we're taking a virtual tour," he says, holding up a DVD.

"What's that?"

"While you were mapping out Bay Front, planning your route for the Green Mission, Dr. Sakata and I visited Four Corners with this in my lap." He opens a thick hardcover book to reveal a space in the middle where pages have been cut away to create a nesting place for a small digital camera. In front of the lens, a peephole has been punched through the book cover. "From the parking garages to the food court, from the day care center to the tanning salon, we covered the mall." He inserts the DVD into his computer and punches a button. "Let's visit Four Corners, shall we?"

For the next few hours we watch the chronicle of Mr. Wells's journey. Nothing's changed much since I was last there, so I'm able to call out store names as the camera travels down the arcades. "Here comes the Gap . . . and Brookstone is next . . . and now Jamba Juice." As we make our way around all five floors of the mall, Mr. Wells points out escalators, elevators, emergency exits and all the doors marked "Employees Only." "Every step of your journey," he advises, "always know your nearest escape route."

After lunch, Dr. Sakata puts me through another humiliating three-hour lesson. Mr. Wells watches quietly as my frustration builds, until Dr. Sakata snatches my wrist for about the hundredth time, and I shout, "I can't do this stupid put-pocketing stuff! Maybe we oughta just scrap the whole White Mission!"

Mr. Wells wheels over, puts a hand on my shoulder and squeezes. "Sam, there's no reason you can't be a terrific put-pocket," he says. "You're the right height, you've got quick hands, and as you proved last night on the Green Mission, you can move like a panther."

I drop my head. "Then how come I suck?"

"Because you lack confidence."

I look up. "Confidence?"

"Dr. Sakata and I both notice that whenever you move in close to your mark, you hesitate. And that hesitation will ruin you." He releases his grip on my shoulder. "Once you can act with confidence, you'll be fine."

"So I've got three days to learn confidence," I mumble.

"You don't need to *learn* confidence," he corrects me. "Anybody who can sneak a Nickel Bay Buck into an idling police car is not lacking in confidence. Now you've got to apply it."

At the end of the afternoon, Mr. Wells hands me a copy of the Four Corners Mall map. "Take this home and study it. Tomorrow, we'll discuss where you'll enter the mall on Sunday, the route you'll take, and how to get you out of there undetected."

I wag a finger at him. "Don't think I don't know what you're doing, Mr. Wells."

"What am I doing?"

"First you sent me to Colodner's Drugstore for the Red Mission. Then, for the Green Mission, you dropped me off in front of that old graffiti I painted, and now you're sending me back to Four Corners Mall." I smack the map against my open palm. "You want me to feel guilty by making me return to places where I've gotten into trouble. I'm right, aren't I?"

"What choice do I have, Sam?" Mr. Wells leans forward. "I can't think of a single shopping area, street or neighborhood of Nickel Bay where you haven't caused trouble, done damage or wreaked havoc. Can you?"

My mouth hangs open until I snap it shut.

"Didn't think so," he says, and rolls away.

When I slip through the hole in the fence behind our garage, I panic at the sound of a lawnmower revving right behind me. Whipping around, I find Jaxon sitting on our stoop, doing one of his impressions.

I laugh nervously. "Good one!" I say, not wanting to let on how he startled me.

"If it isn't Alexander Sam-ilton!" he cries. "What're you doin' out in that alley, buddy?"

"I'm, uh . . . just getting some air," I splutter, and before I can slip Mr. Wells's map under my jacket, he snatches it from my hand.

"Whaddya got?" He reads the cover. "Four Corners Mall? Are you checkin' out the after-Christmas sales?"

"Who's got the money for that?" I laugh as I pluck the map from his hands. "So. What're you doin' here?"

"I hate Christmas vacation!" he shouts, throwing his head back. "It's practically two weeks already, and I've been stuck with my boring family, doing holiday crap the whole time."

"But you're always going to the country club, aren't you?"

"Ack!" he gags. "I'm sick of my dad's country club! And all his stuck-up friends. And when my folks are home, all they do is throw cocktail parties, and after the guests leave, they fight." He punches the snow off a neighbor's hedge. "I finally got away, but now Pincushion says she isn't free tonight—"

I interrupt him to say, "Ivy doesn't like it when you call her that."

"It's only a joke!" He laughs. "Jeez! Everybody's getting so sensitive." He playfully tousles my hair. "So, I figured I'd hang with my man, Sam-I-Am. Whaddya say?"

Eyeing the mall map, I remember that I have a full evening of studying ahead of me.

"Uh . . . I can't."

"Why not?" Jaxon demands.

"Because my dad's dragging me to dinner with his girlfriend and her two brats," I lie.

"What is wrong with you lately?" he asks. "You and Ivy. You're no fun anymore. Hey!" Jaxon pokes me on the shoulder. "How 'bout we go to that bridge over the interstate? We can throw snowballs down at cars and watch them swerve."

"I'd rather not."

"You are such a coward!" he scoffs.

That word hits me hard. Being called a coward right after being told by Mr. Wells that I lack confidence, I have to wonder whether what they're saying is true. Am I really spineless and weak? For a fleeting moment, I consider giving in and joining Jaxon for whatever trouble he wants to get into. But then I remember what Ivy said. *Promise you'll stand up for yourself.*

I raise my chin. "I still think I'm gonna pass."

Jaxon's top lip curls. "Okay. Fine. But you'd better think about what's gonna happen when you return to school next week, Sammy-boy."

"What do you mean?"

"I'm just sayin', you don't want to lose me and Ivy as friends."

"You're going off to high school next year anyway," I remind him.

"So?"

I take a deep breath before I answer quietly, "So maybe it's time I made some new friends."

"Good luck with that," Jaxon sneers. He squints off into the distance, and from the way his jaw keeps clenching and unclenching, I can tell he's mad. Finally he spits in the snow and snorts, "Frankenstein," before he turns and stomps away.

I always wondered who invented that name for me.

Now I know.

THE BUCKS IN THE BOX

January 4

Forget about the day I got my heart transplant or the day Mom left. Forget about the Christmas Day when all this started. The tenth day of Christmas—Friday, January 4—is the worst day . . . *OF MY ENTIRE LIFE!!!!!!!*

And it's all my fault.

As usual I wake up, eat breakfast, take my seven-thirty pill and say bye to Dad as he heads out to work. Through the kitchen window, I can see the gray sky getting cloudier by the minute. After I shower and dress, I review the notes I made the night before on the Four Corners Mall map, and an hour later, as I'm on my way down the alley to Mr. Wells's, my phone plays Dad's ring tone.

"What?" I answer. "I'm kinda in a hurry."

But all I can hear is Dad shouting, "Sam! Sam!" and the sound of other voices yelling in the background.

As I pass under a bunch of power lines, Dad's call gets dropped, but I keep walking, hitting redial over and over again. The line is busy, busy, busy, and by then I'm at Mr. Wells's gate. If I'd only stopped to hear what Dad was calling about, I wouldn't be so surprised by what happens at Mr. Wells's back door.

The first indication something is wrong is that Dr. Sakata won't look me in the face. Even Hoko's head is drooping as he walks beside me into Mr. Wells's kitchen.

"How's it going?" I ask brightly, trying to cut through the cloud of gloom that's hanging over the room, but Mr. Wells simply shakes his head.

"What's wrong?" I look from face to face, trying to figure out what I'm missing here. Mr. Wells taps the TV remote in his lap, and the countertop screen flickers on. What I see makes all the blood in my body rush to my feet, and I have to grab hold of a kitchen counter to keep from collapsing.

The picture onscreen cuts from a shot of the Nickel Bay Bakery and Cupcakery to a shot of my father, smiling like I haven't seen him smile in years. Behind him, customers of the bakery are cheering and clapping as Dad waves a Nickel Bay Ben into the camera.

Okay. You want the truth?

At sunset on Wednesday, as I walked across town to start the Green Mission in Bay Front, you remember how I passed the Nickel Bay Bakery and Cupcakery and peeked in to see Dad waiting on that little old lady? It was after closing time, but he was still in the store, chatting and laughing, doing whatever he could to sell another cupcake and keep his business alive. That's when I noticed—in a corner of the front window—a cardboard sign that had never been there before.

It read FOR SALE.

My breath caught in my throat, and in that moment I knew why Dad had spent New Year's Day at the kitchen table, looking over last year's receipts with bloodshot eyes and holding his head in his hands. Dad was going to close the cupcakery.

My father never told me things were this serious, but then he never really tells me the bad stuff. As much as we fight with each other, he still gets up every morning and bakes all day without ever complaining. Then he comes home every evening to make sure I eat my dinner, take my seven-thirty pill and brush my teeth before bed.

Watching him through the store window, for the first time in my life I found myself thinking, *My dad is a good person.* In that moment, I wished with all my might that I could do something to help him out.

And then I realized I could.

The inside pocket of my jacket was bulging with fifteen Nickel Bay Bens. Who was going to miss one?

I'll admit, what I did next, I'm not proud of. While Dad was still in the front of the shop, I sneaked in the back door, folded a hundred-dollar bill and slid it into the side flap of a pastry box. I froze in place with that box in my trembling hands, thinking, *What're you doing? This isn't part of the Green Mission!* I considered taking back the money and racing out. Nobody would ever need to know I had been there. *But there's a For Sale sign in the window!* my brain was screaming.

Suddenly I heard the front door close and lock. I knew that in the next moment, Dad would come wandering back into the kitchen, and I panicked. I hurriedly set the box back in a stack, slipped out into the alley and ran the rest of the way to Bay Front with my heart kicking like a frightened rabbit's back legs.

When I finish talking, Mr. Wells sighs. "That wasn't the plan."

"I know. I'm sorry. But, Mr. Wells, ever since Nickel Bay Nick returned, you've got me running all over town, giving piles of money away to strangers. Total strangers! Whether they need the money or not!" I look him in the eye. "And then there's my own dad, who's got a For Sale sign in his front window. I saw a chance to help, so I took it. Tell me you wouldn't do the same thing."

Mr. Wells smiles sadly and turns to gaze at the flickering images of Dad on TV. "It appears you've made your father very happy. And with all this publicity, you may have even saved his business." He rubs his face and suddenly looks ten years older. "But you had an assignment, Sam, and you failed to execute it."

I throw up both hands in surrender. "It won't happen again."

"No, it won't," he mutters.

"I promise that, for the White Mission, I will do exactly as you say, no matter what."

"There won't be a White Mission."

I blink. "Whaddya mean?"

"I mean we're done here. We have come to the end of Operation Christmas Rescue."

I gag. "You . . . you can't be serious! What about Four Corners Mall?"

"Not gonna happen."

"But everybody's expecting it!"

"Then won't they be disappointed."

"Mr. Wells, please!" I beg. "I slipped up, okay? But it was just one time. It was one Ben. One single bill."

"One single hundred-dollar bill."

"Okay, so I owe you a hundred dollars!"

"It's not about the money!" Mr. Wells's fist hits the kitchen table so hard that Hoko yelps. "I trusted you, Sam. I trusted you, and you betrayed me."

Suddenly I feel sicker and sadder and worse than I've ever felt. Even worse than when I found out about Mom's new family. To keep from crying, I bite the inside of my cheek until I can taste the blood in my mouth, and I lower myself into a chair.

"You know, for seven years, I acted alone." Mr. Wells's voice trembles as he speaks. "For seven years, I shared my secret with no one but Dr. Sakata, and in all that time, Nickel Bay Nick touched thousands of lives. And *you*—despite your record of arrests and your tough-guy 'I don't give a crap' exterior—I thought that *you* might be honored to share in that legacy. Somehow I thought you could keep our secret. But now . . ." He shakes his head sadly. "Now it's time to put an end to Nickel Bay Nick."

"What?" I cry. "Why?"

"The legend of Nickel Bay Nick has survived because it has always been a mystery. Once the mystery's gone, there's no more magic."

"Who's gonna ruin the mystery?" I ask, frantic. "Not me. I will never, ever breathe a word of this to another living soul."

"You say that now," he grunts, and then wheels toward the kitchen door. I can't let him leave.

"I won't! I won't tell anyone ever!" I can feel tears burning at the corners of my eyes. "I promise!"

He stops and looks over a shoulder. "You promise?"

"I swear, Mr. Wells." I'm blubbering now. "I swear."

He watches me cry, and just as I'm sure that I'm getting to him, he asks, "How can I ever believe you again?"

Thick snowflakes whip through the air as I race across Mr. Wells's backyard. I'm practically hiccupping, I'm crying so hard. Over and over I punch the code into the back gate keypad—*oh-one-oh-five*—but my vision is blurred by tears. Finally I get it right, push through the gate, and dash down the alley, slipping and sliding. I collide with a van that's creeping down the alley with its headlights off. Bouncing off the hood, I stagger to stay upright and keep running while a million thoughts whiz through my brain.

The White Mission is canceled.

Operation Christmas Rescue is over.

Nickel Bay Nick will never strike again.

Back in front of our apartment, I slump to the curb. Folding my arms across my knees, I lay my head down and sob.

If only there were somebody I could talk to, I think. But who is there to tell? Not Dad. Not Jaxon or Ivy. I can't call Mom. And Mrs. Atkinson down at Family Services hates me.

No. I am totally . . . completely . . . hopelessly alone in the world. When my shaking subsides, I'm struck by the silence all around me. With my forehead resting on my wrist, the gentle *tick tick tick* of my watch comforts me and slows down my brain enough that I can start to make a plan.

I've done a lot of damage, I realize, that I have to undo before Mr. Wells will ever trust me again. Where do I start?

I understand now that the money I slipped into Dad's cupcake box wasn't mine to give away. I stole a hundred dollars from Mr. Wells, but what if I return the money? Won't he see how sorry I am for what I did? And then can't things be like they were before?

But I don't have a hundred dollars, and I don't know anybody I can borrow it from. I could probably steal it, but that's the kind of behavior that got me into this mess in the first place. It's at that moment that the ticking of the Rolex finally penetrates my thick skull, and I realize where that hundred dollars is going to come from.

"Mr. Wells, please let me in!" After my repeated ringing of the back doorbell fails to bring Dr. Sakata, I resort to pounding on the glass. "Mr. Wells, can't we at least talk?" What I hear when I stop pounding, though, is very strange.

I hear nothing.

No snarling from Hoko. No footsteps across the wooden floors. From the other end of the house, I can vaguely make out the sound of the garage door closing.

Racing out the backyard and stumbling through the slush in the alley, I sprint out onto Sherwood Avenue, where I veer right. Up ahead I spot Mr. Wells's SUV waiting at the stop sign on Pegasus Lane, ready to turn into traffic. As the car inches forward, I dash into the crosswalk, waving my arms and yelling, "Wait! Wait!" Dr. Sakata slams on the brakes. Fumbling to unstrap the Rolex, I slide around to the passenger side and tap on Mr. Wells's darkly tinted window.

"I got something . . . ," I gasp, dangling the watch where he can see it. "It's worth a hundred dollars! At least!"

With a mechanical hum, Mr. Wells's window descends.

The look of misery on his face stops me cold. "What's wrong?" I ask.

"Hoko is gone."

"Huh?" I step back. *"How?"*

Mr. Wells exchanges a look with Dr. Sakata and then, staring straight ahead, says, "Someone left the backyard gate open."

"Seriously?" I cry out. "Who would have . . . ?" But before the words leave my lips, I know the answer.

"Oh, no," I groan. "No, no, no."

"There's a park he likes on the other side of town." Mr. Wells's voice is flat and cold. "We're going to look for him. I suggest you go home and get out of this weather."

I start to speak, but the window is already gliding shut. Dr. Sakata guns the engine and turns onto Sherwood Avenue. I stand in the street, shocked, until a truck honks, and I stumble back onto the sidewalk.

In the alley outside Mr. Wells's backyard, I turn in circles, trying to piece together what must have happened. Hours earlier, I ran from the house, so upset that I didn't stop to watch the gate close. Something—a twig, a rock— had probably gotten stuck in the gate, and it didn't properly latch. A little while later, Dr. Sakata must have let Hoko out into the yard to run around before the snowfall got any heavier, and the next time he looked out, Hoko was gone.

I study the ground, hoping that paw prints might show which way Hoko went, but enough cars and trucks have

197

passed by that the snow has been churned into a cold, gray soup.

I sag against a fence, devastated as I realize the damage I've done and how badly I've hurt Mr. Wells. All in one day.

Hanging my head, I find a discarded Christmas tree at my feet. Within its snow-covered foliage, I notice something glowing. Reaching through the dried branches, I pull out and sniff at the still-smoldering stub of one of Crummer Sikes's herbal cigarettes. With a gasp, I flash back to the van that I collided with earlier as I ran, sobbing, down the alley.

And suddenly, with the force of a hammer to the base of my skull, the realization hits me, and I know where I'm going to find Hoko.

THE KEY AND THE CAGE

By now, snow is falling in thick clumps and the skies are getting greyer every minute. I zigzag through the slushy backstreets and cut across the seven burned-out blocks of what used to be the Nickel Bay Furniture Works until I reach the warehouse district.

When I see, from a half block away, Crummer Sikes pacing in the alley behind the Nickel Bay Animal Control Headquarters, I skid to a halt and hide. Crummer's van is parked beside him, and even from that distance, I can hear the yapping and meowing from the unhappy strays that he's got locked up in there. I can't pick out Hoko's bark, so I'm not totally sure my suspicion is correct. Until I am, I'm not going to autodial Mr. Wells. Crouching behind a Dumpster in the afternoon gloom, I watch and wait.

For a very long time.

Crummer stomps back and forth, puffing on cigarette after cigarette and slapping at his arms to keep warm. He's clearly growing more and more impatient with every passing minute. Finally a pair of headlights shines down his alley, and Crummer springs into action. Tossing his herbal cigarette aside, he signals—*Come on, come on*—and guides a large black truck up to the back of his van. From the cab of the truck jumps a stocky man dressed in blue jeans and a brown leather jacket. He's got a wool cap pulled down over his forehead and a scarf wrapped up to his chin, so, from my hiding place, I have no idea what the guy looks like. But I can tell you this—he's wearing an eye patch.

The men move quickly. Crummer unlocks one of the nine steel compartments on the back of his van and shines a flashlight through the bars of a cage hardly bigger than a gym locker.

My heart jumps.

Behind the bars I can see Hoko snarling, his dark eyes blinking in fury and fear. Mr. Eye Patch nods as if to say, *Yup, that's the one.*

As much as I want to run to Hoko's rescue, I realize I don't stand a chance against those two guys. I jam my scarf into my mouth to keep from crying out.

Out of his jacket, Mr. Eye Patch pulls what appears to be a thick roll of cash. He peels off one, two, three, four, five bills and hands them to Crummer, who snatches them and shoves them into a back pocket. I didn't believe

Jaxon when he told me that Crummer was stealing rare pets and selling them. Now I'm seeing it for myself.

Mr. Eye Patch rolls up the massive back gate of his truck and pulls a big wire crate out onto the pavement. Crummer slips on thick leather gloves and, from the side of his van, he unclips a long pole with a rope loop at one end. He yanks open Hoko's cage door, and as Hoko leaps to the ground, Crummer slips the noose over his neck and tightens it. Poor Hoko yelps and thrashes at the end of the pole. Mr. Eye Patch swings opens the kennel, and Crummer, with the experience that comes from years of handling angry animals, backs Hoko into it. He slips off the noose and, with one foot, kicks the kennel door shut.

Hoko's pitiful whimpers rip at my heart, but I don't dare break cover. I suddenly remember I should call Mr. Wells, but in the time it takes me to pull out my phone, the men have lifted the cage into the back of the black truck.

Wait! I want to scream. *Don't go anywhere!* But things are happening too fast. Rolling the tailgate shut, Mr. Eye Patch jumps up into his seat, shifts into gear and backs out of the alley as Crummer speeds off in the opposite direction.

I sprint down to Mermaid Street and emerge just as the black truck lumbers past. Mr. Eye Patch steers cautiously as he bumps along the snow-filled, potholed street, so he doesn't notice the jolt I cause when I grab the tailgate handle, swing up and crouch on the rear truck step.

Hanging on for dear life, I quickly devise a plan. Once the truck stops at a red light, I decide, I'll slide the back gate open and pull Hoko's cage out onto the street. I'll be sure to do this somewhere with lots of pedestrians, and when I yell, "Call the police! This man is a dognapper!" I'm confident that dozens of concerned citizens will do just that.

But then I notice the padlock.

When did Mr. Eye Patch snap a padlock on the roll-up gate? My plan doesn't include having to pick a lock! On the back door of a moving truck! And when Mr. Eye Patch takes the on-ramp to the interstate, I realize I'm going to need a whole new plan.

The sun has almost set, and darkness is coming on fast. If not for the heavy snow, passing motorists might notice a small, shivering figure in dark clothing clinging to the back door of a truck, but nobody honks or flashes their lights. The freeway whizzes by under me as I scrunch into a tight ball, and my freezing hands begin to lose sensation. What keeps me hanging on is the fact that, even through the steel door between us, I can hear Hoko barking. Just when I'm sure my fingers will snap like icicles, I catch a break.

Somewhere on the outskirts of Nickel Bay, Mr. Eye Patch exits the freeway and pulls into a neon-lit truck stop. I don't move a muscle until I hear the door slam, and then I drop to the ground and peer around a rear tire.

As Mr. Eye Patch strides toward the 7-Eleven, he unzips his leather jacket and snaps a key ring to his belt.

Mr. Eye Patch is at the front counter when I step up next to him. "Gimme a jumbo grape Slurpee," I tell the round-faced salesgirl. "Please."

"A Slurpee in this weather?" she jokes. "Isn't it cold enough for you already?" She looks to Mr. Eye Patch, expecting a laugh, but he doesn't look up from stirring six packets of sugar into his large coffee. When she sets the Slurpee down in front of me and says, "That'll be three fifty," I take a deep breath and make my move.

"My dad'll pay. He's here somewhere." As I turn to shout, "Hey, Dad!" I grab the Slurpee and sweep it across the counter, right into Mr. Eye Patch's chest. A geyser of purple slush flies as high as the overhead fluorescent lights and comes down all over his leather jacket, wool cap and eye patch.

"You stupid idiot!" he shouts.

"Whoops!" I gasp. With a fistful of napkins, I blot at his jacket and sweater as he swears and slaps my hands away.

"Get offa me! Stop that!" he keeps yelling.

But I just keep wiping and hollering, "I'm sorry! I'm really sorry!"

"What a mess! What a mess!" the counter girl wails between shouts of "CLEANUP AT CHECKOUT!"

Suddenly I spin around to her. "Hey, lady! Where's your bathroom?" Frazzled, she points down a hallway behind the coffee machine, and when Mr. Eye Patch and I both make a move in that direction, I sweep an arm in front of me. "Please!" I tell him. "You go first."

"You're darn right I go first!" he growls as he strides past me and into the men's room.

The second the latch clicks, I block the door with a rack of potato chips and dash out into the parking lot. As I race to the black truck, out of my jacket pocket I pull . . .

Mr. Eye Patch's key ring, which I'd slipped off his belt as I patted him down with napkins.

If only Mr. Wells and Dr. Sakata could see me now! I think as I celebrate with a jubilant fist pump into the cold night air.

With trembling fingers I find the key to the padlock, open it and roll up the back door enough that I can crawl into the truck. Hoko is barking wildly, but when I hiss, "Hoko, it's me!" he stops and blinks through his prison bars. Tilting his head in recognition, he starts to whimper and twitch with such emotion that I almost start whimpering, too.

There's no lock on his cage, I'm relieved to see, but I know better than to open it right away. I've got to be ready for this big dog when I set him free, so I pull off my belt and brace myself. I flick the latch, and the door swings wide.

Hoko knocks me flat onto the floor of the truck, stands on my chest and almost licks off my eyebrows before I can yelp, "Hoko! KO-ra!" Obediently, he sits, trembling all over. I slip one end of my belt through his collar and pull it through the buckle.

Then we make our break.

With the do-it-yourself leash wrapped down my arm and around my wrist, we jump to the asphalt and start to run. Blowing snow covers our footprints as quickly as we make them. A steady stream of trucks pulling into the parking lot provides cover as we race toward the freeway, and once we get there, I look around frantically for somewhere we can hide from Mr. Eye Patch.

Across the freeway, over a bridge spanning eight lanes of traffic, I can faintly see the skeleton of what was once a roadside tavern. Now boarded up and dark, it sits just outside the halo of light spilling from the road sign that announces NICKEL BAY—NEXT THREE EXITS.

My teeth chatter like a tap dancer, so "C'mon, Hoko!" sounds more like "Kuh-kuh-kuh-kuh-kuhm on, Hoko!" As soon as the words leave my lips, Hoko takes off like a shot, dragging me onto the freeway overpass. I try slowing him down, but I'd have more luck stopping a speeding train with a shoelace.

Then the belt starts slipping. The coils wrapped around my arm peel off, until only a single loop remains, straining against the watchband on my wrist. Halfway across the bridge, two stories above all those headlights and taillights, Hoko yanks off that final loop of belt, pulling my Rolex along with it and flinging it high up over the bridge railing. In that split second I have to decide—do I rescue the Rolex or do I grab for Hoko's leash?

My body makes the decision for me.

Lunging, I snatch the leash midair, and I get yanked along, stumbling and tripping. I glance back in time to see my treasured watch sail over the guardrail and drop into the crushing stampede of traffic below.

Heartbroken, I hardly notice that Hoko is hauling me behind the shuttered tavern. With one hand, I struggle to drag him back toward the shelter of the decaying building as, with the other, I try to pull out my cell phone. At that moment, Hoko unexpectedly reverses direction, twisting my arms across my body and spinning my feet under me. Off balance, I teeter for an instant, and then, like a tree toppling in the forest, I start to fall.

For one terrible second I'm aware of the wind howling in my ears and the snow swirling past my eyes as I drop. I can't even tell you what my head hits on the way down.

THE END OF THE LINE

I peel one eye open and see a blurry figure in a wheel-chair across an unfamiliar room. A hollow, faraway voice assures me, "You're okay, Sam."

I look around, trying to make sense of my surroundings as my head swims. "Where am I?"

Mr. Wells rolls up to my bedside. "You're in a guest room on the second floor of my house."

"How'd I get here?" I croak.

"With the help of this." He raises the lid of an aluminum case in his lap to reveal a radar screen. "Hoko is implanted with a microchip that I would normally use to locate him if he were to wander off. The signal won't be detected, however, if he's—for instance—in a solid metal enclosure."

"They took him away in a truck," I explain through parched lips.

"From your location out on the interstate, I assumed as much. But that story can wait." He closes the case and reaches up to adjust the ice bag that's pressing against the side of my head. "Got yourself quite a bump," he says.

Once he mentions it, I'm aware of a throbbing on my scalp. My fingers find an egg-shaped lump above my left ear. "How'd that get there?" I wonder aloud.

"When we found you, it appeared that you had tripped and fallen against a set of concrete steps," he explains. "Hoko was curled up at your side, keeping you warm."

"Where is he now?" I ask. "Is he all right?"

"Yes. Muddy but safe." Mr. Wells nods. "Thanks to you."

"*Thanks* to *me*?" I cry. "But it's all my fault!"

Mr. Wells raises an eyebrow. "Oh?"

"I'm the reason he got out in the first place! I ran out the gate and didn't wait to see that it shut, and then Crummer Sikes came along and kidnapped Hoko and sold him to the guy with the eye patch in the big black truck, and—"

"Sam, Sam, Sam," Mr. Wells shushes me. "Don't get worked up." From the bedside table, he lifts a steaming cup of Dr. Sakata's stinky tea. "Here," he says, "drink this. Then you'll eat a little something and tell me the whole story."

Sitting up, I suddenly feel a cold draft across my body. I raise the covers and am horrified to discover that, except for my underwear, I'm naked!

"What happened to my clothes?" I yelp, pulling the sheets up around my chin to hide the long scar on my chest.

"You were covered with mud and gravel, and soaked to the skin," Mr. Wells says. "We couldn't very well send you home looking like that, could we?"

"So who took off my . . . my . . . ?" I stutter.

"Dr. Sakata helped you out of your wet clothes," Mr. Wells says, and then he holds up a calming hand. "And before you freak out, remember . . . he *is* a doctor."

The warm teacup feels good in my hands. Before he wheels out of the room, Mr. Wells turns in the doorway. "Oh. And your father called while you were, uh . . . resting."

"Is it seven thirty already?" I reflexively look to my watch, but my empty wrist reminds me what happened, and my heart squeezes.

"It's eight thirty-seven," he says, checking his own watch. "I told Dwight you were in the bathroom. Then I apologized for working you so late and assured him that I'd feed you a healthy dinner before I send you home." He holds up the little plastic bag that contains my seven-thirty pill. "Dr. Sakata pulled this out before he tossed your pants in the wash. You can take it with your food."

As usual Dr. Sakata's tea makes me gag, but it does seem to give me a jolt of energy, and the pounding in my skull subsides. After Dr. Sakata brings in my clean clothes, still warm from the dryer, I dress and join Mr. Wells downstairs in the kitchen. Hoko greets me excitedly, yapping and running in happy circles.

"He's super-dirty," I say as I pet him.

"One trip to the groomer, and he'll be good as new," Mr. Wells says.

I eat a few bites of a meatloaf sandwich and hardly touch the bowl of pumpkin soup that Dr. Sakata sets before me.

"Is something wrong, Sam?" Mr. Wells asks.

I set down my spoon. "I lost my watch."

"The one your mother gave you?"

I nod sadly.

"I'm terribly sorry to hear that," Mr. Wells says gently. "I know how much it meant to you."

"I thought it might be worth a hundred dollars," I say quietly.

"Oh, I would certainly think so."

"That's why I wanted you to have it."

"You wanted me to have your Rolex?" Mr. Wells asks.

"So you could sell it. To make up for the money I left at my dad's bakery. Don't you get it?" I lean forward and speak in a rush. "You'd have your hundred dollars back, and things could be like they were, and we could do the White Mission, and I could be Nickel Bay Nick one last time."

Mr. Wells starts to shake his head, but before he can speak, I plunge ahead. "Mr. Wells, I'm really, really sorry, and I want to start over. I want . . ." I choke back a sob. "I want you to trust me again."

Mr. Wells looks at me for a long moment before he asks, "And why is that so important to you, Sam?"

The answer that pops out of my mouth surprises me: "Because nobody else does."

"You're being awfully quiet tonight."

Dad's as happy as a clam, bopping around the apartment, rattling on and on about the steady stream of customers and reporters who keep coming into the bakery. I shove my hands in my pockets and take a deep breath. "Dad? Remember Mom's Rolex?"

At least I can tell him *that* bad news. What I can't tell him is that, despite all my pleading, Mr. Wells still refuses to let Nickel Bay Nick complete the White Mission.

Dad blinks, confused. "Mom's what?"

"That wristwatch you kept hidden in your closet?"

"Whoa. I haven't thought about that thing in years." He shakes his head as if to clear it. "Yeah, what about it?"

I'm ready with my story. "Mr. Wells is really strict about schedules," I explain. "He sends me on errands all over town, and he tells me how long I have to do them and when he expects me back. So I took the watch down from the shelf and started wearing it to keep me on time."

"And you thought *I* was strict." Dad chuckles.

"Just as I was ready to finish work today," I continue,

"I realized the watch wasn't on my wrist. I couldn't figure out where it fell off, so I retraced my steps through the snow all over town, and never found it. Then when I got back to Mr. Wells's, we tore the house apart. And still, nothing."

"Aha." He nods. "So that's why you're late tonight."

"That's why," I lie.

Dad studies my face. "And is that why you're so upset? Because you lost a cheap watch?"

"Dad!" I cry. "It was a Rolex!"

"It was a *copy* of a Rolex." He laughs. "Back when we started dating, your mother bought that at a street fair. As a joke!"

"It was supposed to be valuable," I mutter. "It was her last gift to me." There's a sudden ringing in my ears, and I lean on the kitchen counter for support. As soon as Dad sees my reaction, he stops laughing.

"Oh, Sam, you know your mom," he says gently. "She's always lived in a world of dreams and wishes. I'm sure she *wanted* to give you something valuable. I'm positive. But she didn't have anything to give. Neither of us did. Not back then. We were kids. But I promise you this—if the moon were hers to give, you'd be the only kid on earth with a moon under his bed."

I can't speak.

"Your mother loves you very much."

"Yeah, right."

Dad takes me by the shoulders. "Hey, Sam," he says. "You're the one who won't get on the phone when she calls every week."

"I've got nothing to say to her."

"You could start with hello."

After midnight, the winter storm that had been raging all day really wallops Nickel Bay. The rat-a-tat-tapping of hail on the roof and the clatter of tree branches against my bedroom wall might have wakened me if I'd been able to sleep.

Fat chance.

Staring at my ceiling, I make a top-ten list of all the terrible things that happened in a single day, and you know what ends up at #1? It's not seeing Dad waving the Nickel Bay Buck on TV or hearing that Hoko was missing or clinging to the back of a truck speeding down the highway. It's not even the loss of Mom's Rolex.

Or fake Rolex.

Whatever.

The thing that upsets me the most is that Mr. Wells doesn't trust me anymore.

THE CODE AND THE CUPCAKES
January 5

"Oh, NO!" Dad shouts so loudly from his bedroom that I'm instantly awake.

"What's wrong?" I yell back, but my voice is foggy with sleep.

"That stupid storm last night!" I hear his bare feet pounding as he sprints down the hallway. "We lost power! The clocks all stopped, and I overslept!" Suddenly, he's leaning into my room. "You'd better hurry, kiddo. Don't want to be late for work."

I can't tell him that I don't have any work to be late for. Better pretend it's a day like any other. Throwing off my covers, I holler, "Yikes! How late is it?"

By the time I reach the kitchen, Dad's resetting the oven clock according to his wristwatch. "Seven thirty-five. I don't even have time for breakfast."

He's dressed and ready to go in less time than it takes

me to swallow my morning pill. "Do me a favor, Sam?" he calls from the front door. "Can you reset the rest of the clocks, please? And don't forget the VCR. I'm taping a football game later."

Since I have nowhere to go and lots of time to get there, I eat a leisurely breakfast before adjusting the alarm clocks in Dad's bedroom and mine. It's when I'm resetting the date on the VCR that something truly weird happens.

I punch in January . . . 5 . . . and look up to see

01-05

blinking in the window. "Oh-one, oh-five," I mutter, and then I stop. *Why does that sound familiar?* I wonder. Suddenly it hits me.

That's Mr. Wells's gate combination!

Let me explain why that's such a big deal. Jaxon's been trying to teach me and Ivy to hack into our classmates' Facebook and Twitter accounts using the school computers. "Most people don't want to be bothered remembering passwords and codes, so a lot of jerks use the name of their pet or the date of their birth," he's always reminding us. "If you can get people to tell you one of those things, it's like they're handing you the keys to their lives."

What if that's true? What if those numbers are more than simply Mr. Wells's gate combination?

I throw on my clothes and tear out the door. I think the Nickel Bay Public Library opens at eight.

• • •

A little before noon, Dr. Sakata answers Mr. Wells's back door. I hold up a purple shopping bag and explain loudly, "Delivery for Mr. Wells." At that moment, Hoko dashes out onto the porch and nearly knocks me over with his greeting.

"Hey, Hoko!" I giggle. "I missed you, too."

But Hoko is quickly distracted by a smell coming from my bag, and he buries his head in the sack.

"Hoko! KO-ra!" Dr. Sakata barks, and Hoko immediately sits, panting with excitement. Stepping aside, Dr. Sakata allows me to enter.

We find Mr. Wells in his super-sleek office, studying a computer screen.

"What are you doing here, Sam?" he says coolly when I enter. "I thought I made it clear that our work is done."

"Got a delivery." From my shopping bag I pull a purple pastry box and push it across his desk.

"The Nickel Bay Bakery and Cupcakery," he reads from the cover. "Sam, I'm in no mood to—"

I cut him off with, "Open it."

With a groan, Mr. Wells raises the cover and peers in.

"Those are my dad's three biggest-selling holiday cup-cakes," I explain. "Eggnog, Pumpkin Spice and Pepper-mint Pecan. One for you, one for Dr. Sakata, and one for me. You choose first."

"I don't understand," he says. "There are candles in these."

216

"Oh, yeah. We gotta light 'em. That way you can blow 'em out and make a wish." I watch him carefully as I add, "Isn't that what people do on their birthday?"

Mr. Wells's head snaps up. "I beg your pardon?"

If I wasn't sure before, I'm sure now. "I knew it!" I shout, clapping my hands so loudly that Hoko and Dr. Sakata jump. "It *is* your birthday! And I figured it out!"

He studies me as if he were trying to read my mind, and after a minute his eyes open wide. "Of course. The gate combination."

"Pretty cool, huh?" I say. Mr. Wells smirks, but now I'm pumped. "Come on! You're, like, this big riddle. The man with a thousand secrets. And now I know one of them." I pause before I add, "Or maybe more than one."

"More than one?"

"Didn't you tell me once that information is power? Well, Mr. Wells . . ." I pull up a chair and sit. "I decided I wanted a little more power." He scowls, but that doesn't stop me. "So I spent the morning working on one of those public computers at the library downtown. I Googled things like 'Herbert Wells and U.S. Foreign Service,' or 'Herbert Wells and Southeast Asia,' and I got a couple hits. But neither of those Herbert Wellses had your birthday—January fifth—or a life story matching yours. Just as I was about to bag it, up pops a page about a guy named Herbert *George* Wells."

"Of course. The British author. Early twentieth century. He wrote science fiction, if I remember correctly."

"So you know about him, huh?"

"Why wouldn't I? H. G. Wells is famous."

Exactly what I was hoping he'd say. "Well, that's just it. He *is* famous. As *H. G.* Wells. Hardly anybody knows that the H. G. stands for Herbert George, but *you* do. How come?"

Mr. Wells points to his head. "Just one of those useless facts that clutters my brain."

"I don't think you have any useless facts cluttering your brain, Mr. Wells." I unfold the notes I made at the library. "This H. G. guy wrote some really cool books. *The War of the Worlds. The Time Machine.* Did you know about those?"

"Absolutely."

"Then I bet you know that H. G. Wells also wrote a novel called *The Invisible Man.*"

Mr. Wells grips the armrests of his wheelchair. Now I've got his attention.

"I got to thinking, Mr. Wells. All those years you worked overseas, you had to be a lot of different people, didn't you? It must have been hard—every few years, another country. Another assignment. Another identity. And since you like codes and puzzles, I bet you chose every new alias carefully. You weren't going to call yourself anything as boring as 'John Smith' or 'Bill Brown.' You'd want a name with a little mystery built into it. And I figured that, when it came time to retire in sleepy little

Nickel Bay, you chose a name that contains a clue to the man you've always been . . . the Invisible Man."

Instead of denying my story, Mr. Wells simply gazes at me, unblinking.

"Don't worry," I assure him. "I still don't know your real name. And maybe I never will."

After a tense silence, Mr. Wells nods and says, "No. You won't." Then, with a small smile, he adds, "But now you're thinking like a spy."

So I'm right! I realize, and my pulse races. *Everything I figured out is right!* I try to steady my voice when I say, "It's okay that you're the Invisible Man. I mean, kids at school call me Frankenstein." I point to my chest. "On account of the scar, y'know?"

"That must hurt," Mr. Wells says.

"It used to," I admit. "But not lately."

"Oh, no?"

"Not since I've been Nick." I sit forward and try to put my thoughts in order. "I'd be on a mission, Mr. Wells, and I'd get so scared and excited that my heart would be pounding like . . . like a giant's footsteps. Boom! Boom! BOOM!" I bang on the desktop. "And I'd feel so *alive.* Can you understand? After a lifetime of feeling like I was made of separate parts, finally . . . finally, me and my heart, we were on this adventure together. Like one whole, complete boy. I'd give anything to have that feeling again." My breath catches in my throat, and I can barely whisper, "Mr. Wells, don't you believe in second chances?"

"Second chances?" he gasps, and I can tell I've hit a nerve. But he quickly tries to cover his surprise by asking, "You're still thinking about the White Mission, aren't you?"

I fold my hands in a pleading gesture. "One more time? You and me. Frankenstein and the Invisible Man."

"Oh, Sam." Mr. Wells groans and gazes off into a corner of the room, thinking for a long moment before turning back to me. "Sam. Even if I wanted to go through with it . . . ," he begins, but when I start to react excitedly, he raises a stop hand. "Hold on! Even if I *wanted* to go through with the White Mission—which would have to happen *tomorrow,* let's remember—I'm afraid that, with all the recent distractions, we're simply not ready."

I bounce in my seat. "Mr. Wells, I was born ready. And you admitted yourself that nobody knows the Four Corners Mall like I do."

"Even so," he says with a sigh, "your put-pocketing skills are sadly . . ."

"My put-pocketing skills are awesome!" I exclaim. "Didn't you tell me that if I can learn to be a pickpocket, I can be a put-pocket?"

"I did."

"Well, how do you think I got the key that opened Hoko's truck?"

"I don't know," he responds. "How?"

As Mr. Wells translates for Dr. Sakata, I act out the scene at the 7-Eleven with the grape Slurpee and the hysterical counter girl. And when I get to the part about snatching Mr. Eye Patch's key ring and barricading him in the men's room before running to Hoko's rescue, they break into big smiles.

"You wanted confidence?" I shout, raising my arms like a winning prizefighter. "I got confidence!"

And then they both applaud.

THE MIX-UP AT THE MALL

January 6

It's the twelfth and final day of Christmas, the Sunday before holiday decorations come down and school starts again. On the morning news shows, the announcers predict that everybody in town will be out in public, hoping for their own visit from Nick. "If he's sticking to his usual schedule," says one reporter, "Nickel Bay Nick will make his third and final appearance today. But where he'll show up, nobody knows. So merchants all over Nickel Bay are gearing up for what is expected to be the largest shopping day of the season."

Every security guard at the Four Corners Mall is on duty. Every entrance is being watched by at least eight pairs of eyes. I know all of them, and they all know me, either by sight or from my photo in their computer system. But when I stroll in just after noon, a single ripple in a massive ocean of shoppers, not one of them raises an eyebrow. That's because they're not looking for a short teenage girl in pigtails wearing a Hello Kitty wool cap, lime-green sunglasses, and a pink ski parka with a sky-blue backpack slung over one shoulder.

Don't think "Sam." Think "Samantha."

It was my idea to go disguised as a girl. "To hide in plain sight," Mr. Wells called it. He and I spent yesterday stamping the Nickel Bay Bens and laying out my route. In anticipation of glitches, we created an alternative to the primary mission. "Plan B," Mr. Wells called it. And then, just to be safe, we devised a Plan C. "Although I hope it never comes to that," he said.

Once we decided on my wardrobe, Dr. Sakata shopped, being careful not to buy more than a single item at any one store. He even drove an hour north of Nickel Bay to purchase the brown wig we braided into pigtails. After he returned late yesterday afternoon, I sang a quick "Happy Birthday" to Mr. Wells, and once he made a wish and blew out the candles, we each ate one of Dad's cupcakes.

"Delicious!" Mr. Wells declared, and Dr. Sakata nodded in agreement. Between bites, Mr. Wells warned me that, of all the operations he's devised over the years, the White Mission is by far the most dangerous.

I gulped. "You never said it was dangerous."

"Think about it," he said. "If your cover is blown, you will be chased. If you're caught, a frenzied mob will no doubt tear you apart for the money you're carrying. And what's even worse is that, once your identity is revealed, the entire history of Nickel Bay Nick will be exposed."

My mouth went a little dry when I heard that.

Now, all around me, thousands of shoppers jostle one another while, in the pocket of my parka, fifteen one-hundred-dollar bills crinkle at my fingertips. As anxious as I am to get started so I can finish and get out, I've been warned to take my time at first. "Stroll around," Mr. Wells advised. "Visit every floor of the mall. Watch how the crowds are moving. Make note of places where people seem to be distracted."

Four Corners Mall is built around a soaring central court, which is dominated every December by a twinkling fifty-foot Christmas tree. Riding the escalators and wandering in and out of stores, I observe the crush of bodies at the sales tables in Macy's on the ground level. I study the long lines at the cash registers in Sporting World up on three. And in the food court, I marvel at the two brave souls ordering ice cream sundaes at Baskin-Robbins despite the freezing weather outside. I reconfirm the location of every surveillance camera. And on my journey, from behind my dark sunglasses, I look out at the citizens of Nickel Bay.

Neither of the first two missions, I realize, brought me face-to-face with the recipients of Nick's generosity. While pretending to be interested in the window display at JC Penney's, I watch the reflections of the crowds passing behind me. People are smiling and laughing. They're hugging and greeting one another with a holiday spirit that was impossible to find in this town just twelve days ago.

Suddenly Mr. Wells's final words ring in my ears. "Remember," he warned when he and Dr. Sakata dropped me off four blocks from the mall, "once you actually do start, you've got to move like lightning. The instant someone slips a hand into a pocket or a package and discovers a Ben, the shouting will begin and the mission will end."

Five levels of stores. Fifteen Nickel Bay Bens. That works out to three drops per floor. My mission is clear.

I fight to control the trembling in my left knee and sing a little snatch of Mom's song inside my head.

Now I'm ready
Whoa-oh
I'm so ready!

At Baby Gap on the top floor, in a swarm of bargain hunters, I spy a weary mother pushing a newborn in a stroller as two more toddlers hang on to her. From the back of the stroller dangles a diaper bag, into which I easily slide a Ben.

In Sun & Sand, an older Asian woman on an aluminum walker pauses to squint up at a mannequin wearing a yellow polka-dotted bikini. "Oh, you'd look good in that," I say in a high-pitched voice, and when she turns away, blushing and giggling, I slip a bill into a side pocket of her handbag.

A father and the wide-eyed little boy on his shoulders are entranced by the animated elves in the window at Toys R Us. I casually bump against the dad, mumble "Sorry," as I insert a hundred in his back pocket, and melt into the crowd.

On my way down to the fourth floor, I listen carefully for any sound rising above the hubbub, a joyful scream from somewhere behind me that might indicate the first Ben has been found and the operation is over. So far, so good.

In Slacks 'n' More, as an oblivious guy who looks to be about my dad's age models a new pair of jeans for his wife, I zip into the changing room where his old pants hang on a hook and zip right back out again. Done!

Zip! Zap! Zip! I'm really moving now, my hands flashing in and out of my coat and into other people's pockets and parcels. On the third floor, I steer clear of a pair of security guards making their hourly rounds. Once I'm finished on three, I descend to the second level, where a choir of carolers up on a stage has attracted an apprecia-tive audience. Engrossed in the music, they don't notice the teenybopper in pigtails who squeezes through their midst, leaving Bens along the way.

With only three bills left in my pocket, I'm on the down escalator, heading for the ground floor, when I encounter the first serious threat to my mission. Coming toward me on the up escalator are two pimply teenage boys—fourteen, maybe fifteen years old. One bozo sticks his fingers in his mouth and whistles loudly, as the other one shouts, "Oh, baby! I'd sure like to find you under *my* Christmas tree!"

It takes a second to realize that they're whistling and hooting at me. Not me *Sam,* but me *Samantha.* I stop breathing. As they glide by, the whistler growls, "Oh, mama! What're you hiding behind those sunglasses?" He follows that with a rapid stream of air kisses. "Mwa! Mwa! Mwa! Mwa! Mwa!"

I suddenly regret that I haven't adopted the disguise of a plain Jane, but it's too late now. Is it my fault that, in the right light and with the right wig, I *am* kind of a total fox?

I'm relieved that the yahoos are heading up while I'm going down, but before they reach the top, they both vault over the escalator rail and start to descend, pushing through the bodies in their way. From the steps behind me I can hear irritated shoppers snarling.

"Hey, watch it!"

"Stop shoving!"

"How rude!"

As the stairs slide into the ground floor, I cut through

the mob and make a beeline for the nearest restroom, with my admirers in hot pursuit. My first instinct is to race into the men's room. After all, that's the door I've entered my entire life. But when I remember that I'm in disguise, I whip around and head for the women's room door. Through the thicket of winter coats and shopping bags behind me, I spy my stalkers getting dangerously close, and that's when I realize what a bad move I'm about to make. Those jerks will *expect* me to be in the women's room, won't they?

I spin again, push through the door marked MEN, and nearly trip over a guy who's down on one knee, tying a shoelace. As he's about to look up, I fake a loud, wet sneeze, and he quickly turns his face away from my explosion of germs. I hurry into the main room, where five men and two boys are standing along the urinal wall, busy doing what guys do at urinals. Not one of them glances around. My purple sneakers squeak on the tile floor as I dash into an open stall and lock the door.

Time for Plan B.

Off come the sunglasses, ski cap, wig and pink parka. From my backpack, I pull a dingy-brown zippered sweatshirt, dark-green tennis shoes, a gray scarf and a navy-blue baseball cap. In ninety seconds, I'm Sam again. My shoulder bag turns inside out, so it's now black. Before cramming my old costume into it, I pull the last three Nickel Bay Bens from the pocket of the parka and stuff them into my sweatshirt.

On the way out, I check myself out in the mirror, pulling the scarf up over my mouth and tugging the cap visor down to my nose. There's no question that I'm more exposed, but I feel freer to move around than I did as Samantha.

Hunching my shoulders and ducking my head, I exit the men's room, and sure enough, Tweedle-Dumb and Tweedle-Dumber are pacing in front of the women's room door, waiting to hassle the girl of their dreams. In the blink of an eye, I disappear back into the crush of shoppers.

With only three Bens left, I'm feeling pretty pumped. But as anxious as I am to finish my work and get out of the mall, I'm also feeling a little down. Once the White Mission is complete, I realize, Operation Christmas Rescue will be history. Next year, I'll bet Mr. Wells will be up and walking, and he'll want his old job back. So I have only three more chances to be Nickel Bay Nick. Three more opportunities to feel this frightened and excited.

And complete.

The sight of a security guard holding tightly to the leash of a German shepherd startles me back into focus. *This is no time for daydreaming,* I remind myself.

In front of Bed, Bath & Beyond, a wrinkled old nun wearing dark glasses stands beside a collection kettle, vigorously ringing a bell. Clutched tightly in her other hand is a red-tipped cane, the kind blind people carry. She responds with a cheery "God bless you!" every time she hears the jangle of a coin tossed into her kettle, but I'm happy to report that she doesn't react as my contribution falls silently through the money slot.

A young couple with three little girls—triplets!—gets my second-to-last Ben, and with only a single bill left in my sweatshirt pocket, I pause to look around.

This is it. The last drop of the season. Nickel Bay Nick's final move. What's it gonna be? In the next moment, though, an unexpected sighting makes me gasp and flatten my body against a pillar.

I twist my neck around the corner to see . . . Mrs. Atkinson, my counselor from Family Services. Sitting on a bench in the middle of the arcade, she's eating a hot pretzel with mustard and watching the crowds go by. Instead of wearing her hair in a bun today, she's got it hanging around her face, and the difference is surprising. She doesn't look like the stern, disapproving grump I'm used to. Instead, she looks sort of . . . normal. Pretty, almost. The way my mom looks when she doesn't curl her hair.

At her side sits a girl—her daughter, I'm guessing—a little older than me. Her knees are drawn up to her chest, and her head is bowed over the video game she's playing with great intensity. When Mrs. Atkinson breaks off a piece of pretzel and offers it to her daughter, the girl rejects it with a jerk of one shoulder, not even bothering to look up. A fleeting look of loneliness flashes over Mrs. Atkinson's face, and in that moment, I realize I've never thought of Mrs. Atkinson as a person.

She's always been just another adult in the long line of adults who disapprove of me. She even wanted to take me away from Dad! But seeing her like this—smiling sadly and licking the mustard from her thumb—I get a different impression. Mrs. Atkinson isn't a monster. She's a lady with a tough job who's trying to do what's best. She has her own family, and I can tell she loves her daughter, even if her daughter doesn't get that right now.

I know who's gonna get the last Nickel Bay Buck.

Crossing behind their bench, I zero in on the two shopping bags next to Mrs. Atkinson. Either one of them would make a perfect target. I'm playing with fire, I realize, getting this close to someone who could recognize me, but I'm determined not to wimp out. I rub the final hundred-dollar bill between my fingers, savoring the feel one last time, waiting for Mrs. Atkinson to turn away. A split second of distraction is all I need.

But when it comes, it's not the sort of distraction I'm hoping for.

Behind us, somewhere down the south arcade, a woman screams something, followed by a man yelling words I can't understand.

Every shopper stops. Every head whips around.

I'm so focused on Mrs. Atkinson's shopping bag that I fight the urge to look. Strolling past, I make my drop, and it's only then—once the final Ben is in place—that I actually hear what the man down the hall is yelling.

"Stop him!" he's howling. "Stop that pickpocket!"

Panic rips through my body. *This is it!* screams the voice inside my skull. *You've been caught!* The blood rushing to my head makes me stagger away from Mrs. Atkinson, but the fringe of my scarf snags on a corner of her bench and pulls it from my face. I can't stop to untangle it, because the shouts behind me are growing louder, getting nearer and nearer.

"Don't let him get away!" other voices yell. "Grab that kid!"

Despite the thumping of my heart, I try not to freak out. I lower my head and pick up my pace, plowing through a wall of people. Everyone in my path, though, is stopping, craning their necks to watch the tidal wave of commotion that's bearing down on me. Up above, on the second and third floors, I spot security guards running along the railings, shouting into their walkie-talkies, dashing to the escalators. Then up ahead, without warning, a hulking guard breaks through the crowd, gripping the leash of a snarling German shepherd and running *straight at me*!

Stopping dead, I throw both hands overhead in surrender and am about to shriek, "I give up! You got me!" when the most amazing thing happens.

The cop and his dog run right past me.

Now I'm totally confused. If they're not all chasing me, then who *are* they after? I look back. Up and down the hall, voices are hollering and echoing.

"There he is!"

"Don't let him get away!"

"He's the one!"

I don't see who they're talking about until suddenly, thirty feet behind me, a kid in a hooded sweatshirt sprints out of the crowd of shoppers, leaps over the German shepherd in his path and veers to his right, leading his pursuers down the west corridor of the mall. Just before he disappears from my sight, the hood falls back from the guy's head, and I can see that it's . . .

"Jaxon?" I whisper in shock. *What's he doing here?*

But this is no time to ask questions. Any second now, someone is going to find one of those fifteen Nickel Bay Bens, and then a whole *other* circus is going to break out. And despite the baseball cap pulled low over my forehead, I'm really exposed now. I've got to get out.

I mistakenly assume that every guard in the mall is hot on Jaxon's tail, but when I round the corner to the nearest exit, I find out how wrong I am. Three guards stand between me and the parking lot. And two of them have kicked me out in the past.

With a quick U-turn, I head back into the mall. I was hoping it wouldn't come to this, but I have no other choice.

I've got to activate Plan C.

As I whiz along, I unzip my backpack and, into each trash can I pass, I deposit a single item from Samantha's outfit. When the nylon shoulder bag is finally empty, I ball it up and toss it, too.

Plan C requires me to get myself to the Pampered

Pooch, a pet grooming salon, in the west corridor of the mall. Unfortunately, it's the same corridor that Jaxon has just led all those guards and angry shoppers into, but by the time I arrive, I'm relieved to see the mob has moved beyond the Pampered Pooch. The store's employees—six men and three women, all wearing white smocks and holding hair clippers and brushes—are standing around in the arcade, drawn outside by the uproar. As I slip into the unattended shop and dart into the back work area, I hear one of the groomers asking a passerby, "What's happening?"

"Cops caught a pickpocket," comes the answer.

Twenty minutes later, when Dr. Sakata arrives to pick up Hoko from his grooming appointment, he is led into the workroom, from which he emerges carrying an enclosed kennel. Inside is one shampooed, fluffy dog.

And lying at his side, sharing the crate, is one small boy.

Although I can't see out—and no one can see in—I still hear the footsteps racing past and a new chorus of voices, this time shouting joyfully.

"Somebody found a Ben!"

"Then he's here! He's here!"

"Nickel Bay Nick is in the mall!"

THE CLUE IN THE COAT

On the way home, in the darkness of the dog crate, I calm Hoko by scratching his back, his ears and his neck. He repays me with a thousand kisses. On his collar, I'm confused to discover something hanging alongside his dog tags. I'm rubbing the object between two fingers, trying to figure out what I've found, when suddenly the SUV's tailgate swings open.

We're back in Mr. Wells's garage.

Dr. Sakata unlatches the door of the crate, and Hoko bounds out. I crawl after him, stand up straight and stretch out the kinks. With all the licking I've been getting from Hoko, I'm wet from chin to forehead. I rub my face dry with the sleeve of my sweatshirt, muttering, "Yuck!" which gets an understanding nod from Dr. Sakata. Then I follow him as he carries the empty cage into the house.

A weird grinding sound is coming from the living room, where we find Mr. Wells standing over a paper shredder, feeding documents from the folders on his desk into the steel blades.

"Any problems?" he calls over the noise.

"Nope," I answer. "What're you doing?"

He waits until the machine stops whirring before he answers. "Operation Christmas Rescue is at an end. You have fulfilled your part of our agreement." With the sweep of an arm, he indicates the files and reports he had collected about my dishonorable past. "So now I'm destroying all the evidence I collected on you."

I don't know how to respond. I guess I'm relieved that Mr. Wells can no longer blackmail me, but at the same time, I'm bummed to realize that, yeah, our missions are over. Operation Christmas Rescue is history.

Mr. Wells smiles broadly and rubs his hands together. "So! You had to resort to Plan C, huh?"

For our final lunch together, Mr. Wells decides we should eat in the dining room, so he, Dr. Sakata and I seat ourselves at one end of a table that could easily handle twelve. Then I give Mr. Wells a full account of the White Mission. He chuckles when I tell him about the two boys chasing me down the escalator and into the bathroom.

"Smart move, choosing the men's room!" he exclaims.

When I get to the part about Jaxon, he nods knowingly. "Yes, I heard that on my police scanner," he says. "He's been booked down at the station."

"Dad was right about Jaxon," I grumble, stirring my soup. "I bet his lawyer father gets him out tonight, and he'll be back in school tomorrow." After a moment spent staring into my bowl, though, I set down my spoon and say, "Y'know what I think?"

"What's that, Sam?"

"I think tomorrow, when I go back to school," I announce, "I'm gonna try to make some new friends."

Mr. Wells smiles and nods. "Sounds like a plan."

Without any more missions to prepare for, we linger over our meal. The mid-afternoon sun is throwing long shadows across the dining room floor when Mr. Wells finally reaches into the pocket of his three-button sweater, pulls out a small box and sets it on the table in front of me.

"What's this?"

"Think of it as congratulations for a job well done," he says.

"But I was working to pay you back for the damage to your roof," I protest. "I shouldn't be getting a present."

"It's not really for you."

I scrunch my nose in confusion. "Who's it for, then?"

"Open it and find out."

I lift the lid off the box and fold back the tissue paper to reveal a small wooden picture frame holding a square of glass. It takes me a moment to realize what I'm looking at behind the glass.

It's a coin. A very old nickel. I've seen others like it only twice before. One is in a bulletproof case at the Nickel Bay Historical Society. And the other is in a photo in Dad's scrapbook.

I look up at Mr. Wells. "Is this Phineas Wackburton's fourth nickel?"

"It is," he says. "That's the one your father received from the town of Nickel Bay for saving all those lives in the factory fire."

"But Dad said he lost his! When we moved all those times!" I press my hands to my skull, feeling like my head might explode. "Okay, wait! How . . . how did you get it?"

"Six months after your heart transplant," Mr. Wells begins, "you developed a serious infection. I'm sure you don't remember much of this, it was so long ago."

I shake my head. "It's mostly a blur."

"Your father's finances were already stretched to the breaking point, and the costs of your unexpected hospitalization and treatment were threatening to bankrupt him. He felt that the only thing of value he had was the Wackburton nickel, so, in desperation, he contacted a coin dealer. Who contacted me."

"And you bought Dad's nickel?"

Mr. Wells nods.

"Wow." I lift the tiny frame and peer at the coin. "So, when you asked me to tell you about the naming of Nickel Bay, you already knew the story?"

"More or less, but I needed to learn how much you

238

knew." Mr. Wells nods to the coin. "I thought it might make a nice gift from you to your father."

I look up. "But he'll wonder where I got it."

"So tell him we found it while we were organizing my files," Mr. Wells says with a flip of one hand. "Say that it was in a box with a lot of other coins and trinkets, and that I had no idea what it was."

"Then he'll want to know where *you* got it."

"Oh, Sam!" Mr. Wells chuckles. "You've always been such a good liar. Don't let that skill desert you now!" He rubs his palms excitedly. "You could say that, over the years, I've bought collections from many coin enthusiasts. Tell him that I have been negligent about organizing and cataloguing those coins, to the point that they've ended up jumbled together in a stack of cardboard boxes in my attic. If he asks me, I'll say that I don't remember who sold me what. That story should hold up, don't you think?"

"I guess," I say slowly before I suddenly remember my manners. "I mean, I'm really, really grateful, so thanks. Thanks a lot."

"You're welcome, Sam."

I replace the lid on the box, but my mind is elsewhere. Something in Mr. Wells's story doesn't add up, but I can't put my finger on what it is.

"Mr. Wells? Did you say the coin dealer contacted *you*?"

"I collect historic artifacts." He gestures around the house. "I do business with a lot of dealers."

My eyes narrow. "And that's how Dad was able to pay my medical bills?"

"I assume that's how he used the money." Mr. Wells shrugs. "As I said, I was interested in the coin."

His gaze is steady, and anybody else would believe that Mr. Wells is telling the truth. But now that I'm thinking like a spy, the casual tone of his explanation sets off alarm bells.

"Here's what confuses me," I say, ticking off each point on my fingers. "You just happen to live at the corner of the same street we live on, in a house you happened to move into just after I got my heart transplant, right?"

"If you say so."

"Six months later, Dad's in desperate need of cash, and you *happen* to get a call from the same coin dealer who's selling Dad's Wackburton nickel? Or did *you* call the dealer?"

"It was a long time ago." Mr. Wells tries to sound relaxed. "Does it matter who called whom? Like I said, I was interested in acquiring a rare nickel. I got the coin, your father got the money, and you got the treatment you needed."

"Mr. Wells," I say, shaking my head, "don't you know that it takes a liar to recognize a lie?"

"Why do you think I'm lying?" His voice rises in pitch, and I know I'm getting to him.

"Because!" I explode. "You're not from Nickel Bay! You didn't know me or my dad."

"So what?"

"So why did you help us?"

"I did not set out to help you!" Mr. Wells insists. "You make me sound like a guardian angel."

The breath catches in my throat. "What did you just say?"

Mr. Wells throws his arms open. "I said I am nobody's guardian angel!"

And in that moment, the final puzzle piece clicks into place in my brain.

"Guardian angel!" I shout. "That's it!"

"What's what, Sam?"

Reaching into my shirt collar, I pull out the carving of Hanuman hanging around my neck. "You told me the people of India think of Hanuman as a protector. A guardian angel. Remember that?" I ask, holding up my little statue. "You said it when you asked me how I got mine."

"So?"

"So . . . Hoko!" I call. "C'mere, boy."

Hoko trots over and sits at my knee.

"The whole way back from the Four Corners Mall, I was lying at Hoko's side, getting slobbered over," I explain, "and I was doing this." I run a hand through Hoko's thick coat, and he moans with delight. "That's when I felt something around his neck, something he's always wearing, but it's hidden by his fur, right? I thought it felt familiar, but it was too dark in the cage to see what it was. Then you said 'guardian angel' just now, and you reminded me . . . okay!" I pull the object free of Hoko's fur. "Here it is."

What I'm holding is a duplicate of the Hanuman around my neck.

"Aha!" I shout triumphantly, and lean down so that I can hold my pendant next to Hoko's. "Coincidence? I don't think so. I think Hoko has always worn this."

"But as I . . . as I told you, Sam," Mr. Wells stammers, "people all over India wear Hanuman for . . . for good luck and—"

"And protection," I finish his sentence. "Yeah, that's what you said." I straighten up in my chair. "Last week you asked me to tell you about my Hanuman, but you already knew that story, too. And you knew it because you sent this to me"—I hold up my carving—"in the hospital after my operation. Didn't you?" Instead of answering, Mr. Wells stares at the carving. "And six months later, when I got sick again and Dad needed money, you bought his Wackburton nickel. Only you did it through a coin dealer so Dad never knew you were the buyer." Letting my Hanuman drop to my chest, I lean forward. "So let me ask you one more time, Mr. Wells. *Why were you being my guardian angel?*"

For a long time, Mr. Wells stares at me, until I notice his mouth trembling. Then—and I'm not expecting this— from the corner of one eye, a tear rolls down his cheek. Now I'm really confused. I don't know what I said to make him cry. And I sure don't know how to make him stop.

"He can't tell you himself, so allow me."

The voice comes out of nowhere. It's not me speaking, and it sure isn't Hoko. I spin around in my chair to the only other person in the room.

"Dr. Sakata?" I gasp. "You speak American?"

"You mean English?" he replies, without any accent.

Now my mind is totally blown. *"This whole time?"*

"I live in Columbus, Ohio, with my wife and two children," he says. "I'm head of surgery at the State University Hospital. So, yes, I speak English."

"But why . . ." I gesture between him and Mr. Wells. "Why did you guys only speak Japanese to each other?"

"So we could exchange secrets in front of you. It's a common trick in the world of espionage and interrogation."

Mr. Wells pulls a handkerchief from his sweater and dries his cheeks.

"So what is it," I ask Dr. Sakata, "that Mr. Wells can't tell me himself?"

Dr. Sakata takes a deep breath. "When Mr. Wells's son and daughter were growing up, they rarely saw their father. Depending on where Mr. Wells's work took him, his family was constantly being moved from one exotic location to another, and then he would leave for a top-secret mission, often for months at a time. When he'd return, there wasn't much Mr. Wells was allowed to say to his own children. He couldn't answer their questions about where he'd been and what he'd been doing. He couldn't take them to an office and introduce them to his coworkers. And he was hardly ever around to celebrate their birthdays or Christmases.

"His little girl, Nancy—"

"Is that really her name?" I interrupt Dr. Sakata. "I mean, you guys haven't been exactly honest about *your* identities."

Before Dr. Sakata answers, he looks to Mr. Wells, who makes a little nod.

"That's really her name," Dr. Sakata says before continuing. "Nancy eventually got used to the peculiar arrangement with her father. After all, she had her mother to talk to, and the two of them grew very close. But Mr. Wells's son, Patrick, felt left out, and by the time he was a teenager, Mr. Wells began to notice disturbing changes. Every time he'd return from another mission, he'd find Patrick growing angrier, more distant, more disobedient. Mr. Wells's solution was to send Patrick off to military school."

"I was such a fool," Mr. Wells mumbles, shaking his head.

Now I understand why he flinched when I once asked him, "Did you speak to your own children that way?"

"Instead of changing Patrick's attitude," Dr. Sakata continues, "being sent away to school only deepened his resentment, and after he graduated from college, Patrick cut off all communication with his father. A few years later, Mr. Wells's wife died."

"Do you know," Mr. Wells says with clenched fists, "it

wasn't until Patrick showed up for his mother's funeral that I learned he had gotten married?"

"Oh, that's the worst!" I blurt out. "I mean, finding out someone you love has gone and gotten married without telling you. That really hurts."

Mr. Wells nods. "It hurts deeply."

Dr. Sakata continues. "At the funeral, Mr. Wells and Patrick were as awkward as ever, and Mr. Wells never got the chance to share any of the things he had been saving up to say to his son."

"And Nicky," Mr. Wells quickly prompts him. "Tell him about Nicky."

"Nicky was Patrick's two-year-old son," Dr. Sakata explains. "But when Mr. Wells asked to see pictures of the boy, Patrick insisted that he didn't bring any."

"That's so sad," I say to Mr. Wells. "Have you ever seen your grandson since then?"

The look on his face is one of pure heartbreak. He barely whispers, "A year and a half later, there was an accident."

"An accident?" I look between him and Dr. Sakata. "What accident?"

"One evening," Dr. Sakata says, "a drunk driver ran a stop sign and crashed into the side of Patrick's car."

"No!" I yelp. "Was anybody hurt?"

"It was the strangest thing," Mr. Wells says, in a voice that's dreamy and disconnected. "Patrick and his wife were in the front seat, and they were . . . fine. But . . ."

He opens his mouth, but no words come, so Dr. Sakata continues.

"But Nicky . . . almost four years old at the time . . . he was in his car seat in the back . . . and he . . ." Then Dr. Sakata, too, stops talking.

I shake my head slowly. "I am so, so sorry."

Dr. Sakata takes a deep breath to steady himself. "But, in the hope of saving other lives, Patrick and his wife made the very difficult decision to donate their son's organs."

"That must have been awful," I say. "I mean, I'm only alive today because somebody made that same decision, but . . ."

I stop. A feeling like ice water runs down my spine, and my voice cracks when I ask, "When . . . when did this accident happen?"

Neither Dr. Sakata nor Mr. Wells answers, but they don't have to.

"You don't mean . . . !" I cry out as my hand flies to my chest. "Your grandson! He's . . . here?"

Mr. Wells's eyes squeeze shut and more tears run down his face.

"Omigod, omigod, omigod" is all I can repeat as, beneath my trembling palm, I feel the beating of Nicky's heart.

It takes a while before Mr. Wells is able to speak again. "Of course, the files about the donation were sealed, so it was almost a week before I was able to learn that you were the recipient," he says. "I came to Nickel Bay, not knowing what to expect, and you know what I found? The factory had closed. Jobs were gone. Everyone in town was walking around with their spirits broken. I once bribed my way into your hospital room when no one else was around. And the minute I laid eyes on you, I knew I would have to stay."

"Why?"

"Because, as a father, Sam, I made a lot of mistakes. But standing there at your hospital bedside, watching the machines blip with every beat of my grandson's heart in your chest, I realized that it wasn't just you who was getting a second chance. *I was getting a second chance, as well*. A second chance to make things right. To start again. I had to. Because I couldn't bear the thought of you—with your very special heart—growing up in a town without hope."

The realization floods over me like a sunrise. "And that's why you invented Nickel Bay Nick."

"That's why." Mr. Wells wipes his nose with his handkerchief and wags a finger at me. "But you know what was frustrating? Every year, twelve days before Christmas, I knew how to put a smile on every face in this town. But I could never figure out how to help your father straighten you out. Not until you fell off my roof on Christmas night."

"So I was right!" I cry. "You made me return to the scenes of my crimes, hoping that I'd change, right?"

247

"Did it work?"

I pause to consider his question. "It's a new year." I shrug. "Anything could happen."

None of us speaks for a long time. All the questions are answered. The dots are connected. The mystery is solved. Finally, Mr. Wells looks at the fading sunlight slanting through the dining room drapes. "It's getting late. Your father will be expecting you."

But I don't want to leave. I don't want to walk out of Mr. Wells's home and bring the whole Nickel Bay Nick saga to a close. But I also know I have to go. I've got a life to get back to. I've got school in the morning.

"Will I see you again?" I ask.

"We're neighbors," Mr. Wells says. "Once my cast comes off this week, I'll get back to my old routine. I hope—if you have the time—that you'll occasionally come visit."

"Oh, I'll make the time," I assure him.

"As soon as Mr. Wells is up and walking, I'll return to Ohio," Dr. Sakata says, shaking my hand. "But may I say, it's been a real honor working with you, Sam. You're an excellent student."

"Me, too. I mean, you, too," I stammer. "You know what I mean." I'm still freaking out, trying to remember everything I muttered under my breath in his presence when I still thought he couldn't understand me.

I squat and hug Hoko tightly.

"You scared me out of that tree on Christmas night,"

I tell him. "It's your fault all of this happened." Then I cross to Mr. Wells.

"Congratulations and thank you, Sam," he says, extending a hand. But instead of shaking it, I pull his hand close and flatten it against my chest. Mr. Wells flinches. "What . . . ?" he gasps. "What're you doing?"

"After everything you've done to keep it beating and give it hope," I answer, "isn't it time you felt your grandson's heart?"

And rather than let me see him cry, Mr. Wells bows his head and listens.

THE CHRISTMAS IN THE KITCHEN

The sky reddens as the sun sets, bringing the twelfth day of Christmas to an end. I wait until Mr. Wells's backyard gate clicks shut before I head down the alley.

Back home, I do a lousy job of wrapping Dad's Wackburton nickel in a scrap of old Christmas paper. When I'm done, my stomach rumbles, but instead of waiting for Dad to come home and feed me, I do something I've never tried before.

I start making dinner.

I get the chicken all cut up, but it's not until I'm chopping vegetables that I hear myself softly singing Mom's song.

My heart is strong
My hands are steady
My future waits

And I'm so ready
Whoa-oh
I'm so ready

And without any warning, I suddenly start to cry.

Because I realize in that moment that even though Mom has been hundreds of miles away the whole time, she's been right beside me all along. Her song gave me courage. The pennies from her jar of wishes saved the Green Mission. And even though her Rolex wasn't really a Rolex, it kept me on time.

I haven't really lost her after all.

Dad arrives after dark with two new pairs of jeans and a sweatshirt for me. "We're starting a new year," he says. "I figure that's worth celebrating."

"Cool," I say. And I'm being honest.

"I closed the shop at lunchtime and went downtown to take advantage of the sales," he explains, "but I guess all the excitement was at the Four Corners Mall."

"Yeah, I heard," I say as I keep chopping.

Dad peers over my shoulder. "Are you making my chicken stew?"

"I've been watching you all these years," I say. "I figure, how hard could it be?"

"Well, that's how you learn." He pops a piece of carrot in his mouth, then peers around to look me in the face.

"Have you been crying?"

"Me? No!" I scoff. "The onions got to me. That's all."

Later, when I call him to the table for dinner, he enters, snapping his cell phone shut. "Lisa says hi."

"Hi, Lisa," I say, setting down the two steaming bowls.

"Did you settle things up with Mr. Wells?" Dad asks as he puts his napkin in his lap.

"Yup. Got everything worked out," I answer. "I'm officially no longer in debt."

At that moment, I really want to tell Dad everything about Mr. Wells's grandson and the heart that's beating in my chest. But then where would I stop? I'd have to explain why Mr. Wells moved to our street corner, and why he sent me the Hanuman carving and why he created Nickel Bay Nick and how he picked me to be his substitute this year, and . . . see? It's better that I say nothing.

"Proud of you." Dad lifts his spoon over the bowl of stew. "Now. Let's see how you did," he says before digging in.

"I think I'm gonna call Mom this week."

Dad's spoonful of chicken stops halfway to his mouth. "And say what?"

"I dunno. I'll start with hello."

"I thought you were mad at her."

I shrug. "Yeah, well. I'm over that."

Dad tilts his head. "I bet that would make her real happy."

My stew isn't as good as Dad's, but he praises every

mouthful. Afterward, when I'm putting the dishes in the sink, he starts to stand.

"We're not done yet," I say, turning quickly.

"Oh?" He sits back down. "Is there dessert?"

My heart is pounding so hard, I'm surprised Dad doesn't hear it from across the room. "Sorta," I say. My hands tremble as I pull the badly wrapped gift out from behind the Mr. Coffee and slide it across the table to him.

"I thought you weren't giving Christmas presents this year." He grins.

"We're starting a new year," I say. "I figure that's worth celebrating."

Dad slips off the wrapping paper and lifts the box lid. It takes him a moment to realize what he's looking at, but when he does, he gets very still, and I can see his chin start to tremble. With his head bowed, he starts to ask, "How . . . ?" but his voice catches in his throat.

All evening I've been rehearsing Mr. Wells's story about how the Wackburton nickel ended up in a shoe box in his attic, but I'm only halfway through it when Dad reaches across the table and squeezes my hand. I squeeze his back.

And then I don't have to say any more.